D0488801

DR. MORELLE AND THE DOLL

In a wild, bleak corner of the Kent Coast, a derelict harbour rots beneath the tides. There the Doll, a film-struck waif, and her lover, ex-film star Tod Hafferty, play their tragic, fated real-life roles. And sudden death strikes more than once — involving a local policeman ... Then, as Dr. Morelle finds himself enmeshed in a net of sex and murder, Miss Frayle's anticipated quiet week-end results in her being involved in the climactic twist, which unmasks the real killer.

Books by *Ernest Dudley*
in the *Linford Mystery Library:*

ALIBI AND DR. MORELLE
THE HARASSED HERO
CONFESS TO DR. MORELLE
THE MIND OF DR. MORELLE
DR. MORELLE AND DESTINY
CALLERS FOR DR. MORELLE
LOOK OUT FOR LUCIFER!
MENACE FOR DR. MORELLE
NIGHTMARE FOR DR. MORELLE
THE WHISTLING SANDS
TO LOVE AND PERISH
DR. MORELLE TAKES A BOW
DR. MORELLE AND THE
DRUMMER GIRL
THE CROOKED STRAIGHT
MR. WALKER WANTS TO KNOW
TWO-FACE
DR. MORELLE AT MIDNIGHT
THE DARK BUREAU
THE CROOKED INN
THE BLIND BEAK

ERNEST DUDLEY

DR. MORELLE AND THE DOLL

Complete and Unabridged

LINFORD
Leicester

First published in Great Britain

First Linford Edition
published 2008

British Library CIP Data

Dudley, Ernest
    Dr. Morelle and the Doll.—Large print ed.—
Linford mystery library
    1. Morelle, Doctor (Fictitious character)—
Fiction 2. Detective and mystery stories
3. Large type books
I. Title
823.9'14 [F]

ISBN 978–1–84782–257–4

Published by
F. A. Thorpe (Publishing)
Anstey, Leicestershire

Set by Words & Graphics Ltd.
Anstey, Leicestershire
Printed and bound in Great Britain by
T. J. International Ltd., Padstow, Cornwall

This book is printed on acid-free paper

1

Helen Hafferty stood by the window staring out at the last glimmer of daylight fading from the garden. The trees in the orchard were vague shadows.

He is late, she thought. He had never been late like this before. A vague uneasiness stirred in her and she turned away from the window, letting the heavy velvet curtain fall back into place.

The others were waiting; Helen Hafferty, conscious that she was separated from them by the wall of middle age, watched them grouped round the fire in the wide fireplace with the bookshelves on either side. They were all here, except Nicky her youngest son, and he was unpredictable and moody; but there was Charles, nine years older, and her only daughter, Olivia.

Helen Hafferty's eyes went to Charles' wife, Marie, sitting in the low armchair. Again a sense of uneasiness assailed her.

Marie suddenly looked up and caught her mother-in-law's eye.

'Tod's very late,' she said abruptly. 'Hadn't we better start tea?'

Olivia glanced at her mother. 'I think we ought to wait a while longer,' she said. She got up from her chair by the fire and came over to Helen Hafferty. 'You'll get chilly here.'

Her mother let herself be persuaded to sit near the fire. Olivia's husband, Bill Parker made a polite gesture of offering his chair but Helen Hafferty didn't seem to see him. Instead she sat where Olivia had been sitting.

Bill Parker shrugged and relaxed again. When Olivia came and sat on his knee he began to smooth her thigh with his hand. Her eyes darkened in her thin, once-pretty face and she pushed his hand away. Parker smiled maliciously across at Marie Hafferty, as if expecting his sister-in-law to be amused, but she turned her head away.

Parker sighed. 'I'm not waiting much longer,' he said a little irritably. 'I've a lot of work to get through before tomorrow.'

'Really, Bill,' Olivia said petulantly, 'on a Saturday evening?'

Parker shrugged and his face went mutinous. 'I can't help it if people are queuing up to buy houses. You ought to be pleased. It means money in the bank.'

'Especially,' Olivia added, as if she hadn't heard him, 'after spending all afternoon in the office.'

'He did?' Marie Hafferty looked incredulous.

'Had a whole list of new properties come in,' Parker said, 'just before we left. I had to prepare them for circulation. The sooner our clients know about them, the sooner we're likely to sell.'

Charles grinned his slow grin. 'How you chaps make a living out of buying and selling houses beats me.'

Marie Hafferty said: 'There's a lot goes on between one chap wanting to sell a house and another mug wanting to buy it. Isn't there, Bill?'

Parker gave her an amiable smile. 'That's one way of putting it, Marie, darling.'

Helen Hafferty's voice broke in. 'I can't

think where Tod can be. Perhaps we had better start tea without him.'

'I'll tell Bess,' Olivia said, and she went across to the door. She called down the hall. 'We'll have tea now, please.' A slow, muttered reply reached the others as Olivia came back into the room, and turned to her brother. 'Charles, I think you ought to go out and look for Tod.'

He glanced at her in surprise.

'He could have caught his foot in a rabbit-hole or something,' Olivia said, her thin face worried. 'He'd never be able to get home.'

'There's no way of knowing where he is,' Charles said. 'It'd take over an hour to walk the whole way.'

'You're making a fuss about nothing,' Parker said to his wife. He looked at his watch. 'He must have gone off somewhere. He might have called in to talk to Major Kelly.'

He turned sharply as Marie laughed. 'Come off it; Tod and Kelly? They're poison to each other.'

Charles said slowly: 'She's right though. Tod would never call in on the Kellys.

And there's no one else around here he'd be likely to call on.'

'Of course he hasn't gone to see anyone,' Olivia Hafferty said, her face taut with anxiety, as she gave a look towards her mother. 'It's too bad of you, Charles, arguing, when he might be lying hurt somewhere.'

The other threw down the magazine he'd been reading and pulled himself out of his chair. 'All right. Where d'you want me to start?'

'You'll have to go the same way Tod always goes. Through the orchard and then through Asshe Woods and down to the road, back here. Full circle.'

Charles groaned. 'It's a long way. And it'll be dark in ten minutes.'

'You'd hear him if he was calling out,' Olivia said. 'Anyway you can take a torch.'

Marie said to her husband: 'Want me to come with you?'

He shook his head. He threw a grin at Helen Hafferty. 'If he turns up while I'm looking for him,' he said, 'you'd better send him out again to look for me.'

His mother said nothing as she watched him go out of the room. Marie looked at her, then at Bill Parker, his hand straying over his wife's leg again. He might have gone with Charles, Marie Hafferty thought. She stared back into the fire. And where was Nicky, she wondered? He was always grumbling about his father but he would have gone out to look for him. Or would he?

Thoughts of Nicky made her heart beat faster. The fire was hot against her eyelids. The door opened and Bess was there, pushing the tea-trolley in front of her. Moon-faced Bess Pinner's eyes were like little bright marbles behind their convex lenses, her thin white hair scragged back, showing pink scalp on top of her head.

She said: 'Will that be all, Mrs. Hafferty?'

'Yes, thank you,' Helen said. 'We're starting tea without Mr. Hafferty.'

'Mr. Charles has gone to look for him,' Olivia said.

The convex lenses turned to her. 'Why, d'you think he's gone and got himself lost?' And without waiting for an answer Bess went out, closing the door behind her.

Helen Hafferty shrugged, switched on the big standard-lamp in the corner, and turned to the tea-trolley. The elegant china glimmered, as she arranged the cups and saucers. There was a small dish of thinly sliced lemon; she drank her tea with lemon, instead of milk. Olivia was handing round bread-and-butter.

Marie drank her tea quickly. Where was Charles by this time, she wondered? Searching Asshe Woods with the wind whining through the trees and the grass wet with early dew. She shivered suddenly. The heat and cosiness of the white-painted panelled room suddenly stifled her. She stood up abruptly, her cup rattling in its saucer.

'I'm going to look for Charles,' she said and while they were all staring after her, she hurried out.

Marie Hafferty stood in the hall, a tensed figure, pretty in a plump way. In the light from the small chandelier the white walls crowded with photographs and framed posters glinted. All photos or cinema-posters of Tod Hafferty in the different films in which he had starred, long ago and far away.

Her expression seemed to become curiously tired as her gaze travelled round. From every side his face looked out at her, or he showed his once-wonderful profile; the straight nose, the rounded, cleft chin.

She got a raincoat out of the little cloakroom and went along the passage past the kitchen. She heard Bess Pinner moving about on the other side of the door. A radio was playing. She pulled the side-door open and the February evening, darkening, seemed to flood in. She stepped out into the garden.

She waited until her eyes grew accustomed to the night. Soon she was able to distinguish the details of the garden, the brick path to the small orchard beyond.

This was the way her father-in-law had gone.

On the other side of the orchard a gate opened on to the rough path to Asshe

Woods. That was the way Tod Hafferty took whenever he set out for his walk. Along the rough track and through another gate in the wire-fencing where the woods began. Then on through Asshe Woods to the road, which inclined high enough to look clear across the River Stour towards the old, deserted port of Richborough. Then the road dipped again until it joined the road to Asshe House, Tod Hafferty's home the past seventeen years, since he had brought Helen and his family to live here away from London, during the war.

Three o'clock until around four-thirty, that was the time Tod Rafferty went walking.

Only this afternoon he had not come home.

Marie Rafferty searched the darkness for the gleam of a torch-light that would be Charles returning. She saw it, a will-o'-the-wisp, behind which moved the solid figure of her husband, approaching through the orchard. He had not gone on through Asshe Woods to the road, she thought, and returned by the road, the way Tod Hafferty did. He had not completed the full circle.

She could hear the swish-swish of his shoes through the dew-sodden grass as he drew nearer, and she called out to him.

There was no reply, and a tingle of apprehension ran down her spine. She called again. The moving torch-light halted, and then the end of its powerful beam searched for and found her. She blinked in the glare, and put her hand over her face in an ill-tempered movement.

'That you, Marie?' Charles' voice came to her, with its typical unnecessary question.

'Where is he?'

There was no answer as he stood before her, his face eerie in the reflection from the torch. She could not see the expression in his deep-set eyes, which were black shadows thrown by the torch-light. It was as if he was wearing a pair of dark glasses, she thought, and again that flutter of fear caught at her.

His hidden eyes seemed to be boring into her; she could not see them, but she could feel them. 'Do put the light out,' she said irritably, 'you're wasting the battery.'

He obeyed her instantly, and now she could make out his face as the darkness closed round them. It was a pale oval, blurred beneath the shadow of his hat-brim, and his eyes took on some life, glinting at her.

'Do you think something's happened to him?' she said.

He didn't answer her, and she moved closer to him. His face seemed to take on a tautness, almost as if it was changing shape. His mouth moved, as if he found it an effort to form the words.

'I — I don't know,' he said.

But once more she experienced that tingling presentiment, and she felt sure he was lying to her.

2

Charles Hafferty had left Asshe House, picking up his hat from the hall and pulling his overcoat on hurriedly, struggling with it as he went through the orchard, and keeping his electric-torch moving around from side to side all the time.

His mind was still back in the sitting-room with his wife and his mother, while he felt a vague resentment that Bill Parker had made no effort to accompany him; his brother-in-law was a lazy devil, physically, however alert he might be mentally, he thought. And, he reflected inconsequentially, he didn't like the way he mauled Olivia about in public.

His thoughts turned to his own wife, and the mess their marriage seemed to have become. Lately, he had felt that all Marie was waiting for was something to activate her and she would make some drastic move; walk out on him? He wondered if she would have done it before, if she had been in any position to do so. She had nowhere else to go. She had no money of her own. She was utterly dependent upon him. And things were not all that wonderful with him, his line of commercial art was not paying off so well lately.

It flashed through his mind that perhaps he ought to sell Woodview, the house his father had given him three years before as a wedding-present. It was near Asshe House, and Tod Hafferty had bought it cheaply several years earlier to let to a series of tenants. Wouldn't he do better, Charles Hafferty thought, to sell it and get a flat in London?

Perhaps he would find work easier to get, and certainly Marie would enjoy living in London more than this part of the world. It occurred to him that it was his father who up till now blocked any idea that he might have to get rid of the house. Tod Hafferty would never forgive him for selling his wedding-present.

Charles Hafferty's thoughts fastened on Tod Hafferty and the purpose of this jaunt he was making through Asshe Woods in the darkness, and his jaw set in harsh lines, as he paused and directed the beam of light around him. The trees and undergrowth met his shifting gaze. He had come about fifty yards along the path through the woods, and to his right beyond the edge of the trees was the old chalk-pit.

He turned aside from the path and made his way between the trees until he was clear of them. The chalk-pit was some twenty strides ahead. The ground was rough, and already his shoes were wet through. He glanced a little uneasily at his torch, he fancied it had given an ominous flicker. He hoped the battery wasn't due to pack up, or the bulb. He didn't relish finding his way back to Asshe House in the darkness. But the light now seemed as strong as ever. It was only a momentary anxiety.

He made out the void of the chalk-pit a few feet ahead and proceeded cautiously. Now he reached the edge and flashed his torch downwards into the darkness.

It was as if some magnet drew the

torch-beam at once. It fastened on what lay in the centre of the circle of light, as Charles Hafferty stared down, then with a quick movement, he turned, made his way along the edge a couple of yards and found a way down the side of the pit.

A few minutes later, he scrambled back to the chalk-pit edge, where he stood for a few moments getting his breath again. Then without a further glance down behind him, he directed the torch-beam ahead and made his way through the woods again.

He went through the gate in the wire fence, then, walking more quickly now, along the rough path until he reached the gate to the orchard. He went through it, and it was then that he thought he saw a figure in the darkness ahead.

He thought it was a woman's figure and decided it must be Olivia who had come out after him. When he heard Marie call out to him he experienced a twinge of surprise. His mouth felt dry, so that he couldn't answer her. He moved more quickly and heard himself mumble her name, then she was there in the light of his torch.

There were her questions, then she was telling him to save using up the torch-battery, and he was answering her he didn't know what had happened to Tod Hafferty, and they were returning to the house.

'He'd raise the roof,' Marie was saying, 'if we started a search and it turned out he'd been somewhere he didn't want anyone to know about.'

'Some woman?'

'I didn't say so.' Charles Hafferty shrugged his thick shoulders. 'How far did you go?' she said.

'Through the woods, then along about a quarter-mile. I didn't go any further along the road; if he'd got hurt there, he'd have been found by passers-by.'

She nodded. 'D'you think that's what's happened? That he's in the woods and hurt? There are some bad places.'

He muttered indecisively.

They paused, looking out across the orchard, the blackness accentuated beyond the torch-beam with which Charles Hafferty kept searching the darkness.

'Should I get Bill?' he said.

'A fat lot of use,' she said. 'He'd be afraid of getting his feet wet.'

They listened to the hiss of the wind blowing in from Sandwich Flats.

At last: 'Ought we to tell the police?'

It was Marie who spoke, and her husband let out his breath in a long sigh. 'Telling a copper, just because someone's late back from a walk?'

'They'd know what to do,' she said. 'Whether to start searching or wait a little longer.'

'I suppose so.'

'We could phone, and see what they said.'

He gave her a nod, then he turned and went back to the house. She followed. They went in by the side-door, shutting out the night with a slam.

Tea had not yet been cleared away. Anxiety hadn't diminished anyone's appetite, Marie thought, noting the emptied plates; Bill Parker was cramming a piece of bread-and-butter in his mouth. Olivia was halfway through a slice of fruit-cake.

Only Helen Hafferty sat staring across the room, her cup of tea and lemon untouched beside her.

All eyes came up to Charles. He said flatly: 'I didn't find him.' He looked across at his mother.

'Think we ought to get on to the police?' she said.

Bill Parker choked, until tears started into his eyes. Olivia made a vaguely protesting noise. Her mother stood up and moved to Charles, standing uncomfortably in the centre of the room.

'What do you think?' she asked him.

He had always been her favourite, Marie thought inconsequentially. Maybe it was because he was so quiet and steady, not moody like Nicky, and Olivia, too, she could be a little morose at times.

'It wouldn't do any harm to give them a ring,' Charles said, awkwardly. He added unconvincingly: 'They would know the drill.'

Bill Parker had recovered his composure. 'I don't think it's anything to bother the police with,' he said. 'You're making a mountain out of a molehill. If a man can't go off on his own without everybody chasing round trying to find him . . . ' His voice trailed off.

Charles Hafferty looked at him stolidly. 'He's my father.'

'If you mean I don't care what happens to him, that's nonsense,' the other said. He got to his feet, covering a slight belch with his hand. 'I'm as concerned about him as much as everyone else. Only I think you're in too much of a hurry, that's all. He'll turn up soon, and then we'll look fools.'

Charles Hafferty looked at Marie, then across at his mother. 'Shall I ring up?'

His mother's voice trembled a little. 'If you think it's best.'

It was Olivia who gave Charles the telephone-number of the local police-station, and Bill Parker looked up at her sharply as if surprised she should know it. As Charles moved to the hall, the door opened and Bess was there to clear away the tea-things. She stood silently watching Charles as he went into the hall.

They could hear him lift the receiver and ask for the number; then a pause.

Then he began talking to someone the other end.

Trust Charles to get it all back to front, Marie thought irritably, as he stumbled his way through his account of how Tod Hafferty had gone for his walk. Good job the local cop to whom she supposed Charles was babbling on knew the Hafferty family quite well, she thought. He'd be able to fill in the gaps her husband was leaving.

They heard the click of the receiver replaced.

Charles Hafferty was perspiring a little as he came back into the room. They could see the perspiration shining on his face.

'Well?' Marie rapped at him.

'He's going to report Tod's disappearance to the police-station at Eastmarsh. He'll call out here as soon as he can.'

'And then?' Bill Parker asked.

'Then we'll start a proper search,' Charles said. He crossed to Helen Hafferty, who stood, her face stiff, her slim figure tensed. 'Unless — ' He broke off and then said unconvincingly: 'Unless Tod turns up before the cop does.'

3

P.C. Frank Jarrett had promised himself a quiet Saturday evening. A few official reports to clear up, then some reading, and early to bed. Charles Hafferty's telephone-call had caught him with his shoes off, his toes curling before the fire. P.C. Oxley had answered the phone in the office and then came back to the sitting-room.

'This sounds like yours,' he said.

When he hung up, Jarrett came back in his socks, and began to put on his shoes again. Oxley's eyebrows went up. 'Trouble?'

'Old man Hafferty,' Jarrett said. 'Gone and got himself lost, or something.'

'Tod Hafferty?'

Jarrett nodded. 'Seems he hasn't got back.' He reached for his overcoat. 'I could do it in a couple of minutes on your motor-bike,' he grumbled.

'Maybe they'll reconsider it after your

last report,' Oxley said. 'You knocked up enough miles, last month.'

Jarrett went out of the warm sitting-room, muttering over his shoulder at this arbitrary allocation of motor-cycles. If that lot over at Sandwich had to manage on a push-bike they'd soon change their ideas.

A few minutes later he was riding out of the handful of houses and cottages which comprised Eastmarsh, along the road towards Asshe. By now his head was no longer full of the inconvenience of having to use a bike instead of Oxley's motor-cycle; his thoughts revolved round the business of the previous afternoon, and the couple he had kept an eye on, and which had haunted him ever since.

When P.C. Jarrett had first noticed the girl and the way she wore her flashy clothes, a way well ahead of her years, which made her technically at any rate under the age of consent, he had thought it would not be long before she caught some male roving eye. But he had not expected that it would turn out to be the man he had seen her with six weeks or so ago.

There may have been others before him, but Jarrett knew nothing about that.

He didn't require much experience to realize that this sort of case was difficult to handle. It would have been the last sort of job he wanted to take on, anyway, but the identity of the man complicated the whole thing even further.

He had seen him and the girl on three or four occasions after the first one. Once under the shelter of a hedge, then, a haystack, the edge of a cornfield; he had watched them once disappear into a clump of bushes.

But until he saw them yesterday afternoon, when he was off-duty, in plain-clothes, on their way to Eastmarsh railway-station, he had no evidence to support his suspicions. It was in the middle of the Friday afternoon at an hour when passenger-traffic was slack; and it seemed to him that an empty railway-compartment was probably just the job for the man and the girl.

Jarrett had followed them to the

booking-office while the man bought two returns to Sandwich. He kept unobtrusively close behind the pair on the platform.

When the train came in he saw, as he had expected, that it was less than half-full, and again as he had anticipated the pair got into an empty compartment just as the train was about to move out. There was another empty compartment immediately next to theirs, and Jarrett nipped in as the guard blew his whistle.

To obtain the evidence he needed he realized he would have to leave his own compartment, step on to the running-board of the train, now travelling at speed and observe through the next window what was taking place.

He lowered the window of the right-hand door of his compartment, opened it, grabbed the hand-grip which is provided for the cleaners when the carriages are in a siding, and stood on to the running-board. He eased himself clear of the door as he closed it from the outside, making certain that it was fast, and then, changing hands, swung himself a foot or so forward, when he should find himself level with the window of the next-door compartment.

He accomplished the manœuvre without much difficulty. The man and the girl occupied the seat with its back to the engine, and his first glance told Jarrett all he needed to know to charge the man.

It was then that it occurred to him to take a look to see that the line ahead was clear, and two hundred yards off, he saw a tunnel. The train was doing forty miles an hour, and he knew that he couldn't escape being struck by the wall of the narrow tunnel.

There was no time to regain his own compartment. There was nothing left for him but to remain where he was. The tunnel appeared to be rushing towards him while he remained hanging on to the hand-grip. The tunnel yawned at him, a vast and appalling menace, swelling to a gigantic size until he could make out the mortar between each brick.

The daylight disappeared like a light suddenly switched off. The acrid stench of smoke filled his nostrils, the thunder of the racing wheels became a deafening uproar. Stones displaced from the track cracked against the tunnel-wall like pistol-shots.

He felt the brick-work grazing his back and shoulders while the escaping steam from the pressure-pipe beneath the running-board blinded him. After what felt like an eternity he was once more in the daylight, and the train was rattling along steadily. He was still there.

Eventually he got back into his own compartment, and collapsed into a corner, and looked at his clothes. One trouser-leg was half-torn off. His raincoat was split down the back. He was black with soot from head to foot.

But what worried him most was the problem of what he should do about the evidence he had. He could go into court now and describe with convincing detail what he had witnessed taking place between the man and the girl; it would be enough to send the man to jail.

But P.C. Jarrett had done nothing about it.

He had got out of the train at Sandwich

and without waiting for the two in the next compartment he had crossed over to the other platform, managed to clean himself up a little, and then caught a train back to Eastmarsh.

His duty was to have charged the man on the spot, but he had not done so. He had kept the entire business to himself, not even mentioning it to Oxley.

And now here he was dragged out over the very man he ought to have pinched yesterday afternoon having gone and got lost. The girl was the daughter of an Eastchurch layabout, a no-good who'd done time for house-breaking.

The man who had been with her was faded film-star, Tod Hafferty.

By now Jarrett had passed the bunga-low, a long and low brick-built building called The Nest, which stood back from the road with a wide drive leading up to it. It was masked by tall trees, except for a low, white swing-gate. Jarrett glanced over the gate as he rode by, glimpsing the comforting light from the windows. This was where the slightly mysterious Profes-sor Kane lived alone, with a housekeeper, a middle aged little woman, to look after him.

Two hundred yards further on, P.C. Jarrett passed the Kelly's place, converted from two farm-labourers' cottages. The name on the iron gates under a brick arch was Roselands; in the summer the front-garden was filled with roses. But Jarrett's interest whenever he passed was less for the picturesque house or Major Kelly or his wife, but more for Fay Kelly, their daughter. If only he wasn't an ordinary village cop, he had told himself often enough, he might have chanced his luck with her.

She had given him one or two long, smiling glances when they had encountered each other, and he had felt his heart beat somewhat faster.

Another hundred yards or so, and he was passing Woodview, occupied by Charles Hafferty and his wife. He frowned to himself as he brought his mind to bear on business. He knew that Charles Hafferty was some sort of commercial artist whose efforts, Jarrett imagined, could hardly be coining money;

but the pair of them appeared to be reasonably well-off.

The life of the locality, with its slow rhythms, held little appeal for P.C. Jarrett. The mesh of human activity, not the pattern of the rural year, stirred his interest; people, not the village-fêtes or flower-shows, the local football-teams or darts-championships, aroused his concern and a feeling of responsibility. People like Tod Hafferty and the rest of his family. Charles Hafferty's house was in darkness, Jarrett saw as he rode past. He and his wife would be down at Asshe House waiting for Tod Hafferty.

Curious if the old boy had gone off somewhere, instead of going home. Jarrett's mind went back to the railway-carriage episode. Had he been with that girl again, and something happened which he had not bargained for? Jarrett also wondered what his family knew, if anything, about his carryings-on. Mrs. Hafferty, for instance, did she know, or suspect?

He reached the double, ornamental iron gates of Asshe House, with a shoulder-high wall on either side. He left his bicycle propped against the wall, went up the short, wide flagstoned path and rang the bell. The light was on in the hall, he saw, as Bess Pinner opened the door to him. She stared as if he was a ghost, though she had seen him often enough.

'Will you come in, please?'

He stepped into the hall, looking curiously about him at the walls smothered with the photographs, film-stills and posters. He had been a keen film-goer and remembered seeing Tod Hafferty in a number of films; and then some of them had been shown lately on television, which Jarrett had chanced to see.

Marie Hafferty came from the sitting-room, smiling brilliantly at him. Despite himself his eyes travelled quickly over her, the sweater too tight and showing the nipples of her breasts, the hip-hugging skirt. Why did she dress that way, he thought? She looked like a plumper version of the kid he'd seen with her father-in-law. Who was there to impress? Her brother-in-law, Bill Parker? He was a bit of a bottom-pincher, by all accounts.

So Tod Hafferty had not returned.

'So kind of you to come so quickly,' she said. 'My husband will be here in a moment; he's just reassuring his mother. She's become very upset, I'm afraid.'

P.C. Jarrett pulled off his overcoat and with it over his arm and clutching his helmet, he followed Marie Hafferty across the hall. She opened the door and they went in. The dining room was white-painted, with a dark, polished refectory-table, a welsh-dresser with rows of pewter jugs and dishes, and china plates hung on the walls.

Jarrett was aware of Marie Hafferty's vitality, the scarcely controlled animal energy that seethed in her as she stood beside him. She made him feel very young and uncomfortable. When she caught his eye she smiled coolly.

'What do you think could have happened to Mr. Hafferty?'

'Difficult to say. The chance is he may have had an accident and be lying helpless somewhere.' He looked at her. 'Could he have gone off by himself without letting anyone know?'

31

'Doesn't seem like him,' she said.

Charles Hafferty came into the room. He was still wearing an old duffel-coat and had put on rubber boots. His face was set in grim lines, his small, deep-set eyes anxious. His face relaxed when he saw Jarrett. They talked briefly, her husband explaining how he had already made a quick search, while Marie watched them, and Jarrett noticed she was smiling that disconcerting, secret smile. She hardly seemed aware of her husband.

'You'll want to cover the ground your father would have taken this afternoon,' P.C. Jarrett said to him.

'I went as far as the chalk-pit when I went out,' Charles Hafferty said. 'Then I turned back. I felt I needed help to look properly.' He turned to Marie. 'We won't be long, we hope.'

She turned suddenly to Jarrett. 'Can't I come with you? I can see like a cat in the dark.'

Her husband said quickly: 'You're better indoors. Somebody ought to stay with mother.'

'That's Olivia's job,' Marie said. 'She's her daughter, not me.'

'Will Mr. Parker be coming with us?' Jarrett said hastily.

'Not likely,' Marie snapped. 'He and his wife took very good care to nip off before you arrived. Tramping about in the dark isn't Bill Parker's idea of fun.'

It wasn't his idea of fun, either, Jarrett thought; a curious sense of oppression filled him, making him feel anxious to get away from this house. An atmosphere of unhappiness had gathered around them as they stood there.

'If you want rubber boots there's an extra pair in the kitchen,' Marie Hafferty was saying to him. 'I daresay they'd fit you.'

She led the way through the hall. In the large, bright kitchen, where the radio was playing, Bess found the rubber boots and Jarrett pulled them on to replace his own shoes. They came up to his knees and would be useful. There would be a soaking dew for certain. Bess took charge of his shoes and he followed Charles Hafferty out of the kitchen-door. Bess had told him the rubber boots were used by the daily handy-man, Alf. P.C. Jarrett knew Alf Layton. 'Alf's got pretty big feet for a shortish man,' Bess said, 'but I daresay they'll be all right.'

A minute later he and Charles Hafferty were heading towards the orchard, their powerful torch-beams picking out details from the surrounding darkness. They came to the end of the orchard, went through the gate and made for Asshe Woods, and the chalk-pit.

4

At 3.30 p.m. that Friday Miss Frayle had kept an appointment with her dentist at the Wigmore Street end of Harley Street. It was a matter of a wisdom tooth which she had been putting off for several weeks; and then it had begun to give her rather more intense pain, and she had forced herself to do something about it.

Tomorrow, Saturday, evening she was accompanying Dr. Morelle on a weekend visit he was making to a friend in Kent, and the last thing she wanted was to have any trouble with the tooth while she was away from London; she had no difficulty at all in picturing Dr. Morelle's impatience with her if that happened.

This was something she had not failed to point out when she had explained to him why she had to interrupt her work for an hour that afternoon, and he had grumbled that he was in the middle of a batch of notes he wanted to dictate to her.

Miss Frayle had indicated the tape-recorder in the corner of his study and left him to it.

She was terrified at the prospect of visiting the dentist, and made no bones about telling him repeatedly from the moment she took her place in his chair. He smiled at her reassuringly and then began explaining that she would need rather more than a local anæsthetic.

'Just an intravenous injection,' he said.

'You mean, I'll be unconscious?' she gulped, the palms of her hands wet with perspiration as she gripped the smooth arms of the chair.

'You won't feel a thing,' he nodded.

Terror flooded her; but almost without her realizing it a white-coated figure had appeared at her side; he was Dr. Someone-or-other, the dentist was murmuring, who as it happened had arrived a little earlier than expected to give a pentathol injection to a patient whose appointment followed Miss Frayle's.

Miss Frayle fixed him with a sickly

smile as the man said: 'Lucky I was here.'

She remembered reading only that morning a newspaper report of some old woman dying in a dentist's chair; and then she nearly fainted dead away, as she caught the glint of a hypodermic. Everything was happening so swiftly, so slickly, if only she possessed the courage to make a dash for it. Then she had a mental picture of the mirthless amusement on Dr. Morelle's sardonic features as he listened to her if she had to tell him what had transpired.

Somehow the picture of him in her mind gave her a kind of desperate courage.

The cool-looking brunette nurse was smiling at her soothingly as her arm was bared, and the anæsthetist was bending over her. She closed her eyes. 'Start counting,' a voice was saying. She opened her eyes, she hadn't felt the hypodermic, but she began counting.

'One . . . two . . . three . . . '

Now she couldn't have kept her overweight eyelids open for a million pounds.

It was somewhere about five-thirty that she had found herself and Dr. Morelle in a first-class compartment of a Southern electric train snaking through the darkness of the winter's evening, and she tried to puzzle out why they were travelling down to Kent by train, when she had understood earlier that Dr. Morelle would be using the Duesenberg. She leaned forward to speak to Dr. Morelle, wreathed in smoke from his Le Sphinx, but he was too immersed in his book for her to risk interrupting him, and she snuggled back in her corner.

'We are travelling by train, instead of by car, because our arrival will be less conspicuous.'

For a moment Miss Frayle didn't grasp that Dr. Morelle was speaking to her. His attention seemed to be concentrated on the page before him, and he did not look up. Then her eyes widened as she realized that he had read her thoughts.

'Oh,' was all she had been able to think of to say. She frowned to herself. Why should their arrival have to be so secret? 'I thought we were just paying a weekend visit — '

He interrupted her, still without looking up from his book. 'The object of our journey is to meet Tod Hafferty.'

The name had rung a bell. Wasn't he some actor or someone? Miss Frayle dug into her memory. Yes, that was it, he had been a star in pre-war British films. He had gone out to Hollywood, where he had proved to be less successful; then he had returned to England to appear less and less frequently in roles of less and less importance. Then no more had been heard of him. A has-been, she indexed him in her mind, that was what he was.

'But why Tod Hafferty?' she had said. 'I never knew he was a friend of yours. Or is he a friend of — ?'

Dr. Morelle had put down his book and spoke through a cloud of cigarette-smoke. 'He is not the only individual with whom I expect to be concerned.'

Miss Frayle blinked at him while he gave his attention back to his book. She couldn't imagine what possible interest he could have in an ex-film star. Besides, she thought irrelevantly, Tod Hafferty must be at least sixty. She wondered if he was married. She glanced at Dr. Morelle. Was it something to do with Tod Hafferty's wife? Was that what he had meant by his cryptic remark?

She leaned forward again. 'Who else, then?'

At that moment the train screamed into a tunnel, and her question was lost. She started to ask it once more, then decided to wait until the train was out of the tunnel. She eyed the solid blackness outside the compartment-window, which threw back her own reflection at her. She shifted her gaze along until it fastened on Dr. Morelle's reflection.

Then the train was out of the tunnel and the darkness of the night opened out again, the lights of houses, of street-lamps and car headlights racing past formed an enigmatic pattern.

'Who else, then, Dr. Morelle?'

'Have you forgotten Carlton?'

She stared at him blankly. His dark gaze narrowed beneath his jutting brows raked her from over the cover of the book he was reading. With a start she saw the title. *The Life And Loves of Tod Hafferty*, it said; she could not make out the name of the author.

She seemed to recall that there was something scandalous about the ex-film star, some notoriety which he had brought upon himself. She wondered idly if it was this which had been responsible for the failure of his career.

She tried to recollect what it had been, what scandal had caught up Tod Hafferty and ruined him, but whatever it was, it escaped her. She looked at Dr. Morelle with rising interest. Was he interested in some case involving Tod Hafferty?

She started to question him about his apparent concern for the ex-film star, and then she remembered that he had mentioned someone named Carlton. Where did Carlton come in?

'Who's he?' she heard herself saying, and then broke off with annoyance as Dr. Morelle lowered his book once again, and now she could see clearly under the title that it was by Derek Carlton.

He was tapping the book. 'The author of this, of course.'

'But I still don't see what either of them have got to do with you. Tod Hafferty or, or — ?'

'Don't you?' He was smiling at her thinly. 'Look in your handbag.'

Automatically she obeyed him, opening it without taking her eyes off him; she saw his glance fix itself on her hands clutching her handbag, and she looked down. It was empty, except for a gleaming hypodermic-needle.

Then it was as if she was gazing into some dark whirlpool, she could hear a voice very near. It wasn't Dr. Morelle who was speaking; as she opened her eyes, the dentist was bending over her.

'That isn't likely to trouble you again, Miss Frayle,' he was saying.

'Oh, hello?' she said. 'I was having a fantastic dream.'

He smiled at her sympathetically. 'Hope it was a pleasant one.'

She nodded vaguely. She began trying to puzzle it out. The journey in the train; Dr. Morelle reading his book in the corner. Then she said: 'How long was I unconscious?'

'Not long. You didn't require another shot. It was a nice, easy extraction.'

She nodded again, this time smiling wanly. She felt thankful it was all over. A surge of elation filled her, and she sat up in the chair. The anæsthetist had gone; the brunette nurse was busy in the background.

She stood up, the dentist's hand at her elbow to steady her. She felt a little shaky, but pretty good. No pain where the wisdom tooth had been.

'Feel all right?'

'Perfectly,' she said.

Ten minutes later, he was escorting her along the thickly carpeted hall to the front-door. She was assuring him she would not require a taxi to take her the short distance back to the other end of Harley Street. He opened the door for her, while he asked her to convey his kindest regards to Dr. Morelle.

The door closed behind her and she stood at the top of the marble stairs which took two flights down to the street.

Beside her were the ornate gilt and black liftgates. She started to walk down, when the dentist's words of greeting to Dr. Morelle echoing in her head made her stop. She turned back to the front-door and looked at the neat brass plate over the letter-box.

Derek Carlton, the name was. That was his name. She had thought it was Derek, though she hadn't noticed it particularly before.

She started downstairs again, frowning to herself. It was easy to understand why the reference to him had appeared in her mind while she was unconscious, though why as the author of *The Life And Loves of Tod Hafferty* was a bit fantastic. As fantastic as the idea of Dr. Morelle being so engrossed in the book, or in some case involving some faded film-star named Tod Hafferty, whom Dr. Morelle would never have heard of.

Miss Frayle was smiling a little as she began walking up Harley Street. Tod Hafferty? She began searching her mind in an effort to remember when she had last seen him in a film.

She thought of the work which lay ahead of her; there was more than enough to be cleared up before she left with Dr. Morelle on this weekend visit tomorrow.

5

Charles Hafferty and P.C. Jarrett pushed on silently, each peering out to the perimeter of his pool of light. The grass was soaking, it had been a heavy dew all right, as soon as darkness fell. It was rough going up to Asshe Woods; once Jarrett nearly twisted his ankle. The rubber boots were a size too big.

As they came up to the rough track, the wind sighed through the tangle of bushes and trees, and Jarrett saw the white outlines of the gate which the man beside him was indicating. 'That's the way my father goes,' he said.

He unhitched the gate and they went through. A cheerless spot on a wintry evening like this, Jarrett decided, with a shiver. To their left a tangle of blackberry and thorn bushes and beyond it the black leafless trees. Where they stood was a small clearing, then the woods and further along, P.C. Jarrett remembered, was the chalk-pit, an unsavoury place full of rusted tin cans and rubbish.

'Straight through the woods,' Charles Hafferty was saying, 'and out the other side. But that's not to say he did the same today.' Jarrett didn't say anything. 'I mean,' the other went on, 'he didn't get home, so something must have been different, somewhere.'

'Shall we look at the chalk-pit?'

'He didn't usually go that way.'

'You just said he must have done something different today,' Jarrett said. Charles Hafferty caught the faintly triumphant grin beneath the shadow of the helmet, and he nodded.

'You've got a point there, too,' he said.

Jarrett led the way; he crashed forward through the tangled bushes, blackberry thorns ripping at his coat, his torch-beam casting wavering shadows. They reached the chalk-pit at a place where there had once been a wire fence, but it was now a tangle of rusty, broken wire strands.

A wicked place, Jarrett thought, standing as close to the edge as he cared to. Ought to be properly fenced off. A danger to children. The pit fell steeply down, its sides a jungle of bushes and debris; it had become the cemetery of rusted petrol or diesel oil cans.

The two torch-beams flickered over a holed bucket, an ancient iron bedstead, a battered pram, a twisted mess of chicken-wire.

Charles Hafferty said abruptly: 'He's not here. Better get on. It's quite a way if we're going all round.'

They turned away and started along the track that led through Asshe Woods.

Whippy branches caught at them, patches of leaves that concealed dips in the path caused them to stumble. Charles Hafferty keeping his gaze to the right, the other to his left, they pushed on. The leafless trees creaked in the wind, the surroundings assumed the quality of a dream.

P.C. Jarrett fell into a reverie, Marie Hafferty's image jumping up disconcert-ingly in his mind.

A dangerous, discontented woman, he thought. Not the kind of wife he'd care to take on. How did Charles Hafferty cope with her? His thoughts switched to the task before him; it was beginning to look a little serious, Tod Hafferty's failure to return home for his tea.

When they emerged from Asshe Woods at the other side, the wind hit them in a sudden squall, so that Charles Hafferty gasped and shivered.

'If he *is* hurt, and stuck out on a night like this, it will give him pneumonia, at least.'

Jarrett murmured sympathetically. From where they stood he could see the lights of the Kellys' house. Inviting lights on a chilly night. Only one light upstairs, Frank Jarrett noticed. Somebody sitting in their bedroom. Fay Kelly, he wondered romantically, alone and lonely?

He and his companion, who seemed to have become withdrawn and kept nervously glancing behind him, as if he had forgotten something, gained the road. They proceeded along it for a hundred yards, the road inclining slightly all the way. They paused. From this point, as they stared out towards Sandwich Flats, the darkness opened out across flat, marshy terrain, cut twice by the River Stour doubling back on itself. The wind was fresh in their faces, tasting of the sea. Behind them and to their right lay fields and wasteland, and Asshe Woods, through which they had come.

Jarrett realized, with a hopeless shrug to himself, that he and Charles Hafferty had kept to rough track and path all the time; Tod Hafferty could have strayed anywhere on the route he habitually took, beyond the searching light of their torches. He might have pushed on in the direction of the derelict harbour at Richborough, or a score of other points. Or he might merely have turned off the road along which they were now heading, back towards the handful of houses known as Asshe.

It wasn't much of a search they were making of it, but it was the best they could do. Jarrett hoped fervently the old chap would be back at Asshe House when they returned. He and his companion went on; he sensed that Charles Hafferty felt equally that they were wasting their time.

Soon they were proceeding slightly downhill to reach the wider road at the foot of the decline, which ran between Asshe and Eastmarsh, the way P.C. Jarrett had biked earlier that night.

When at last they were back at Asshe House, they stood looking at each other in the darkness, their faces pale in the glow from their torches.

'At least we know he isn't lying up there with a broken ankle,' Jarrett said.

The other said nothing, and led the way to the house. He pushed the kitchen-door open and Jarrett followed him into the warmth. The radio was still playing. Bess was sitting by the table. A local newspaper was spread in front of her, but she was not reading. Her convex lenses came up to them.

'You didn't find him?'

'We've been all round,' Charles Hafferty said, 'and he's not there.'

Bess shook the white hair combed flat and pulled into a knot in the back of her neck. Jarrett and Charles Hafferty pulled off their rubber boots and put on their shoes.

'We'd better break it to Mother,' Charles Hafferty said.

Jarrett followed him to the hall, and then into the sitting-room, with the fire blazing comfortingly in the wide fireplace. Olivia and Bill Parker were not there; no doubt they'd thought it unnecessary to call in again about the lost man. Marie Hafferty looked up from the book she was reading, and Helen Hafferty jerked her head and her eyes fastened on her son. She had been sitting staring into the fire.

'We've been all round,' Charles Hafferty told her, 'and he's nowhere to be found. Not to worry, it must mean he's gone off somewhere and he's bound to phone, or else turn up here.'

His mother looked from him to Jarrett, who nodded reassuringly. 'I'm sure he's nowhere outside, Mrs. Hafferty,' he said. 'We'd be certain to have seen him.'

'Would you?' Marie said. 'On a night as black as this?'

Her husband swung round on her; Marie's eyes gleamed, then he turned back to P.C. Jarrett. 'What happens now?'

'Nothing more I can do at the moment.

52

Mr. Hafferty might still turn up any time. I'll go off now, and I'll give you a ring later on.'

Charles Hafferty glanced again at his wife. 'Looks as though it'll be best if I wait here.' She didn't answer him. He turned to Jarrett. 'What time will you ring up?'

Jarrett eyed his watch. It was nearly 8 p.m. 'I'll give him till 10.30. Then if he still hasn't come home we'd better try again.'

6

P.C. Frank Jarrett shared the living accommodation at the Eastmarsh police-station with Oxley, who was married, and whose wife was away for a week visiting her family in North London. During her absence a neighbour came in to do the cooking and look after the house. At the back of the police-station Jarrett kept his Alsatian dog, Hero, in a properly built kennel and where there was plenty of space for training-purposes.

Jarrett was not only a dog-lover, and thought Hero was the most intelligent and courageous dog ever used for police-work, but he also received a weekly allowance for training and handling him.

He took Hero with him at night whenever he went out on his beat which did not require him to ride his bicycle. This was not so much that in the event of any trouble the dog would prove useful, but more to give him exercise and keep his training up to standard. Hero was a one-man dog; no one else other than Jarrett handled him.

He had learned that a dog was a useful companion when his beat took him on foot round the outskirts of Eastmarsh, or along the banks of the River Stour. As well as defending his handler or tracking criminals on the run, a police-dog should be able to find anyone lost, or injured and awaiting rescue. So far, apart from scaring off a few tramps, Hero had never been put to the test; but tonight he was getting his big chance.

There was no news by 10.30. Jarrett phoned through himself to check that Tod Hafferty had not, in fact, turned up. Charles Hafferty answered the phone. No, there was nothing from his father. He had sent for the odd-job man at Asshe House, Alf Layton, to come and help look for him, he said. Jarrett mentioned he was bringing the dog.

Normally, Oxley would have been out on his beat, but tonight he remained at the police-station while Jarrett went off. Without Mrs. Oxley, there was no one to take any emergency calls.

With Hero off the leash at heel, Jarrett set out to make a brisk walk of the two miles from Eastmarsh to Asshe.

It was when he was a quarter-of-a-mile from Asshe House that he saw a figure outside The Nest. He saw by the light of the torch that it was Professor Kane himself by the gate, and as he felt Hero hesitate beside him he spoke a quietening word to the dog, then called out a greeting.

'I'm waiting for friends, down from London,' Professor Kane explained. He was a youngish, tubby man, who had lived at his bungalow, it was part laboratory, for several years, working on some secret research, according to local gossip, or something very hush-hush. Jarrett had seen him once or twice over at Richborough's forgotten, silted-up harbour.

'They were delayed in London,' Kane was saying, 'so didn't leave till late. All the same, they should be here by now. Hope they haven't got lost.'

He glanced at Hero, and then questioningly at Jarrett.

'Talking of people getting lost,' Jarrett said, 'that's why I had to bring him out tonight.'

'Who is it?'

Jarrett, usually a discreet man who kept his mouth shut, thought there would be no harm in telling the other about Tod Hafferty's failure to return from his afternoon walk. Kane said he had a nodding acquaintance with Hafferty; he made little comment, Jarrett noted, apart from a conventional expression of sympathy, and the policeman wondered if the missing man's amorous inclinations were more in the nature of a public secret after all.

Had the sordid carryings-on with the girl got anything to do with this business about his not returning? It was a question which kept nagging at the back of his mind.

'I don't think Dr. Morelle is the sort to lose his way,' he heard the tubby man beside him say, and he jerked a look at him. The other caught it, and gave a little smile. 'Of course, you'll have heard of him, I'm sure.'

P.C. Jarrett certainly had. So this Professor Kane was a pal of the great Dr. Morelle was he? Perhaps the work he was engaged on was something pretty important, after all.

'Is he down for the weekend?'

'Yes; with Miss Frayle, of course.'

Jarrett made up his mind to keep a look-out for them. He had read plenty about Dr. Morelle in police-journals and the newspapers; seen photographs of him leaving the Old Bailey, or in the company of Scotland Yard top brass. And once or twice, he had seen Miss Frayle photographed at parties, with Dr. Morelle in the background. A pretty little thing, Jarrett recalled, with horn-rimmed spectacles.

'I'll keep a look-out for his car,' he said to Kane, as he made to continue on his way.

'You won't miss that,' Professor Kane said, 'even in the dark. It's a great yellow monster.'

P.C. Jarrett, with Hero padding at his heels, continued on his way.

A hundred yards further on the

headlights of an oncoming car swung round the curve in the road. It was proceeding slowly, as if the driver was looking for somewhere, and Jarrett guessed this would be Dr. Morelle. He waved his torch, signalling the other to slow down. As the car drew nearer, the policeman felt sure his guess had proved correct. In the reflection of the massive headlamps, he saw that it was a rakish, low-slung yellow Duesenberg. He was a bit of a fan of vintage cars, and the dramatic lines of the car slowing up filled him with admiration.

A face which he recognized leaned out. 'Anything the matter?'

P.C. Jarrett glimpsed the young woman beside the gaunt figure at the wheel; her horn-rims were turned towards him questioningly, and he heard her say, rather unnecessarily, he thought: 'It's a policeman, with a dog.'

'Didn't want you to get lost,' he said pleasantly. And he went on: 'Professor Kane's bungalow is about a hundred yards along.'

'I know.' The answer he got was not

quite what Jarrett had expected. 'Is that what you stopped me to tell me?'

The cold tones matched the hard gleam of the dark eyes in the shadow of the hat-brim. Jarrett gulped.

'I — yes — that is, I've just left him, and he told me he was expecting you, Dr. Morelle. He wondered if you'd lost the way.'

'I never lose the way.'

'Oh, Dr. Morelle,' the young woman said reprovingly. 'What about — ?' She broke off. 'Never mind. It was very kind of you,' she said to Jarrett.

'A pleasure, I'm sure, Miss Frayle,' he said.

He saw her eyes widen behind her spectacles. 'How did you know it was me — ?'

P.C. Jarrett thought Dr. Morelle was about to say something, as he replied: 'I've seen your photo, of course.'

'Oh,' she smiled at him from the darkness of the car, and he thought she had a very sweet smile. 'Not on one of your Wanted posters, I hope?'

'Thank you,' Dr. Morelle said to him

coolly, as he released the brake and the Duesenberg moved forward again. 'You have been most helpful. I hope you find the man you're looking for.'

Jarrett caught Miss Frayle saying something to the effect that it was a lovely dog, and then the car was gathering speed and its headlights were tunnelling the darkness in the direction of Professor Kane's bungalow.

It was only when he reached Asshe House that the thought occurred to him. How the devil had Dr. Morelle known he was out looking for someone lost? And then he realized that Dr. Morelle had been even more specific than that; he had known it was a man who was missing. Not a woman, or a child.

Jarrett was still puzzling over it, when he arrived to find Charles Hafferty awaiting him in the light from the hall which threw a pool on the dark path. He was all ready, wearing a heavy coat, scarf and rubber boots. He noted that Jarrett was also wearing rubber boots, his own this time.

'Alf has just gone to change his boots,'

he said. What about Nicky Hafferty, Jarrett wanted to know, and was told that he had not yet returned to Woodview, where he chose to live with his brother and sister-in-law. Nor had Bill Parker offered to join the search. Not much of a search-party, Jarrett thought, and it seemed to him strange that Parker shouldn't want to help find his father-in-law. The excuse that he had a lot of work from his office to deal with sounded thin. Still, sons-in-law didn't always care much for their fathers-in-law, he supposed.

Alf Layton slumped out of the darkness at the back of the house, buttoning an old army overcoat over what appeared to be a variety of pullovers and scarves.

He was short and stocky, and Jarrett saw the gleam of excited anticipation in his eyes. This would be worth several pints to him at his local tomorrow. By that time he'd have convinced himself he had organized the whole thing.

Jarrett turned to Charles Hafferty. 'We shall want something of your father's. A jacket, something like that. The dog has to get the scent.'

Charles Hafferty looked a little surprised as if he didn't quite understand the request, then he said: 'I'll see what I can find,' and he disappeared into the house.

Alf rubbed his woollen-gloved hands together. He sniffed the air, looked round at the sky and trees. 'Going colder, it is. Shouldn't wonder if there's a frost before morning. Wind's dropped too.'

P.C. Jarrett had scacely noticed the weather. Now with a slight shock he saw how the night had changed. When he and Charles Hafferty had made their first search the wind had blown chill and damp. And there had been neither moon nor stars. Now the moon was riding clear of the clouds and a few faint stars were showing.

He remembered his earlier trudge through Asshe Woods and the rest, and he glanced at Hero. 'I don't like it,' he said. 'All that heavy dew at dusk. There won't be much of a scent.'

The jacket Charles Hafferty brought back was old and tweedy with leather patches at the elbows. It was one his father had worn in the very last film he had appeared in, he told Jarrett, who looked suitably interested. That was why the old boy had hung on to it all that time. 'He still has ideas of getting back into pictures, that's my belief,' his son said. 'Frustration, that's his trouble.'

Jarret could not help recalling his behaviour with the girl in the railway-compartment. He hadn't appeared so frustrated, Jarrett thought. He held the jacket to the dog's nose. 'Take a good sniff, Hero,' he urged. 'Then go find.'

The dog nuzzled into the cloth of the jacket, then made a low sound in his throat and turned for the open gate. Jarrett wound the end of the leash round his wrist and went after the dog. The others fell in behind. The Alsatian went straight through the garden, sniffing eagerly, and on into the orchard. Jarrett could hear Alf Layton talking in a low voice to Charles Hafferty.

Suddenly Hero stopped, nosed around, then stopped again. The men stood waiting. Alf Layton whispered: 'He's found something,' but Jarrett shook his head.

'He's lost the scent. It's no wonder. The grass is soaked with dew.'

The dog was turning in circles, sniffing, trying one way and another, making small urgent noises in his throat.

'Pretty near talks, he does,' Alf Layton said. 'Probably he's asking us which way to go next.'

Jarrett turned to Charles Hafferty. 'We could try further along if you like. See if he can pick it up again.'

'What about the woods? More dryish stuff on the path, perhaps.'

'It's worth a try. Come on.'

P.C. Jarrett tried to sound enthusiastic, but he became aware for the first time of an overwhelming fatigue. They were wasting their time, he felt certain. Hero would never pick up the scent once he'd lost it. The three men followed the dog through the gate in the wire fence and into Asshe Woods.

There were some patches of leaves where the dew had not fallen, and P.C. Jarrett led the way, Hero alongside, thrusting through undergrowth which ran on both sides of the track that led from one end of Asshe Woods to the other. He stopped in a small clearing where a fallen tree lay like a rustic bench.

Jarrett had been carrying the jacket rolled up under his arm. Now he held it to the dog's nose and repeated the urgent command: 'Go find, Hero.'

The dog circled the clearing, nose down, searching for the man's scent.

'Set him off along the path,' Charles Rafferty said, and Jarrett pulled the dog on to the track and began to walk along it, as Tod Hafferty usually walked along it. After a few moments he gave it up.

'Scent's gone,' he said. 'Heavy dew.' Alf Layton muttered something, as if he understood the impossibility of the dog getting anywhere.

'No point going on?' Charles Hafferty said.

'Trail is cold. Best thing we can do is go home and turn it in; we aren't doing anyone any good out here.'

Charles Hafferty stood kicking the path with the heel of his rubber boot, his face set and heavy. Jarrett felt suddenly sorry for him. What he had said might be right, but his way of putting it sounded a bit callous. He was tired and worried that there was nothing that could be done about anything, now.

The trio turned back to the gate where they'd entered the woods. They tramped back through the wet grass, with the Alsatian quiet and relaxed at Jarrett's heel.

As they reached the road to the orchard of Asshe House, the moon sailed out from behind a bank of clouds and the trees in the orchard ahead suddenly came into focus, no longer vague blurs in the darkness, but rows of branchy skeletons. P.C. Jarrett happened to glance back in the direction of Roselands. It was a good distance away, but in the clear moonlight, and from where he stood, he could see across the side-wall at this end of the house's garden.

The moon was riding clear and the whole scene was flooded with a cold brilliance. Suddenly he picked out the figure in the garden. It was a woman, he could see that. Which of them was it? Mrs. Kelly, or Fay? And what was she doing in the garden late on a cold February night?

The figure turned away. He saw the pale blur of a face looking in their direction. The woman must be asking herself what was going on, dark figures and torches flashing in the woods.

Alf Layton's inquisitive voice spoke in his ear. 'Something wrong? You seen something?'

'No, nothing.'

Concerned for some reason that he could not name, that the other should not see what he had seen, Jarrett turned and walked quickly. Charles Hafferty was pushing on ahead. Alf trotting beside Jarrett muttered confidentially: 'What d'you think's happened to him? Hopped it somewhere and not told nobody?'

Jarrett ignored him; he had no intention of discussing it with Alf Layton. But the man tagged along, muttering away. He wouldn't be surprised if the old boy had a lot of irons in the fire he didn't let on about, he said. Look at the way he went off on his own whenever he felt like it. To Sandwich and Ramsgate, Margate and Broadstairs. He named the places as if they were Babylons of sin and iniquity. After all, he'd been one of those film-stars once; he couldn't be blamed if he went after a bit more lively company than the locals.

At the door of Asshe House, Jarrett turned to Charles Hafferty. 'Sorry about this, but you saw how it was.'

'Nothing more you could have done.' Charles Hafferty looked at the dog, panting on the end of his leash. 'Might as well all get to bed.' He took the rolled jacket from Jarrett, who pushed his helmet aside to scratch his head dispiritedly. 'I'm sure he's nowhere nearby, anyway.'

'There's nothing more we can do tonight,' Jarrett said. 'I'll telephone Sandwich and we'll have his description circulated first thing. If he hasn't turned up by the crack of dawn tomorrow, we'll have another go. We shall be able to make a proper search by daylight.'

Charles Hafferty glanced up at a lighted window. He turned to Jarrett and nodded, his face weary and anxious. 'It's

Mrs. Hafferty I'm worried about.'

'He'll turn up,' Alf Layton said with an attempt at conviction. 'I'm sure we couldn't have missed him up there.'

But Jarrett knew how easy it would have been to pass someone lying in the undergrowth of the wood, unconscious, without the help from Hero, on account of the dog being unable to pick up any scent.

The thought of the long, cold walk home was intolerable. He was too weary even to begin it. His own warm bed seemed impossibly remote. He could not believe he would ever be lying with the blankets pulled up to his chin, and sleep washing towards him like a slow tide.

A few minutes later he was heading along the ribbon of the road, bathed now in moonlight, Hero padding along at his heel. He had left Alf Layton to change back to his ordinary boots; and Charles Hafferty had said he would phone him if there was any news during the night.

Passing Woodview, he noticed a light in an upstairs window, and the image of Marie Hafferty passed across his mind.

Her husband had mentioned to him that she had gone home, leaving him to remain at Asshe House for the rest of the night, in case of news about Tod Hafferty, and anxiety for his mother. Once again, P.C. Jarrett experienced that disturbing sensation when he thought of that plump brunette, with her too-tight sweater and round, wiggling behind. And that odd, secret little smile of hers. Just as if, Jarrett reflected, she was cheating on her husband, and was getting a smug kick out of it.

Only, who with? Who was there around these parts that Marie Hafferty could pick as a secret lover?

He was probably maligning her, Jarrett decided; she was really as good and faithful a wife as any man could want. Just because she was a bit sexy-looking didn't necessarily mean she was that sort at all. It was the quiet ones, the ones who dressed as if they were going to Sunday-school, with shy, reserved personalities, who often turned out to be the nymphomaniac type.

He frowned to himself. Human nature

was a dicey business and no mistake, only he felt too tired to worry about it now.

He had gone about thirty yards past Woodview, with the picture of the upstairs lighted window still photographed at the back of his thoughts, when he heard the tap-tap of high heels approaching. Out of the shadows of the skeleton-branched trees ahead, he saw a figure emerge, and he paused, then kept going.

P.C. Jarrett could feel his pulse quicken as he saw the face caught in a pool of moonlight. He saw her hesitate as she caught sight of him. Then she came towards him.

It was the girl he had seen with Tod Hafferty in the railway-compartment.

7

Half-a-dozen ideas for action sped through
P.C. Jarrett's head as the girl drew nearer.
This could be a chance to find out if she
knew anything about Tod Hafferty's vanishing-
trick; he could ask her point-blank or merely
inquire helpfully if she was looking for
some house, and lead up to the other
matter. Or she might give it away that she
did know something about the old boy,
where he had got to, and why.

But supposing she played it tough,
clammed up on him? Pretended she
didn't know what he was talking about,
had never heard of Tod Hafferty? He
could imagine the sort of talk she would
give him, if she chose to take that line. As
he eyed her now, he told himself she was
the sort who might even try and turn the
tables on him by screaming out that he
had attempted to molest her. Or something equally nasty for him to explain
away. Especially as he had kept quiet

about what he had witnessed between her and the missing man — if that came up he would find himself in a spot.

But what the devil could she be doing over here at this hour? Her home was a couple of miles away in Eastmarsh, where she ought to be in bed. He could only suppose she had come out, hoping to see Tod Hafferty; or, it occurred to Jarrett, to learn if his failure to return from his walk had started things humming. Assuming, that was, that she was aware he had disappeared.

'Good-night, P.C. Jarrett,' she called out, as she passed him, her eyes gleaming in the darkness as she gave him a sidelong glance.

He could only mutter a reply, and hear her high heels tap past, sensing that she kept looking round to see if he was glancing back. There was nothing he could do about it, he argued, it was no business of his if she wanted to take a late-night stroll in Asshe. A great wave of weariness swept over him, and he shook his head with a sense of inadequacy; he had missed an opportunity, he felt certain, even if he could not shape in his mind precisely what the opportunity added up to.

P.C. Jarrett trudged on, Hero padding along at heel. When he had proceeded some twenty-five yards, he paused in the shadow of an overhanging tree, to stare back. He could not make out the girl's figure, though he thought that the click-click of her heels fading in the gloom came back to him. He stood listening, peering through the darkness, but he could not see her; and the faint noise of her heels, if he really had heard it, had died away. Silence, except for the whisper of wind in the branches; and somewhere beyond Eastmarsh the rattle of a train.

He did not move, but debated the idea of waiting until she returned; he assumed that she would get back to her home some time that night. But supposing he did wait for her, what would he gain by it? If he hadn't been able to stop her and question her then, why should he feel more capable of doing so later?

Besides, he ached with tiredness. All he

wanted to do was to fall into bed. He began moving again, his chin sunk in his collar, his eyelids heavy with sleep. He could fall fast asleep as he walked, he felt.

He found himself wondering all over again if the girl might know something in connection with Tod Hafferty's disappearance; and he began to plan a way of contacting her, without arousing her suspicion. But his brain was so tired he couldn't even recall the girl's name, though he knew he had heard it.

He caught the creak of a gate ahead, and his eyes came up with a jerk. His weariness left him, as if wiped off a slate, at the sight of Fay Kelly walking towards him. She had obviously just come out of the garden of Roselands. It was she and not her mother he had seen earlier, on his way back from Asshe Woods, he decided. The figure in the moonlight then had been wearing a jersey and skirt. This was what she wore now, beneath the open raincoat.

Jarrett wondered if Fay Kelly had seen the girl go past. Was that what had brought her out? But he could not think why she should be interested in the girl. She knew nothing about her and Tod Hafferty. Or did she?

It was an odd coincidence, encountering the two girls within the space of a few minutes on the same stretch of lonely road. He couldn't attach any significance to it. It was just a trifle odd, that was all. Another thought occurred to him. Why had Fay Kelly been in the garden watching them returning from their fruitless search? She knew nothing about Tod Hafferty's disappearance.

His tangled conjectures were interrupted by her quiet query: 'What is happening?' She came closer to Jarrett. 'What were you all doing in the woods?' She stared at the dog and then looked at him sharply.

'Old Mr. Hafferty. He's been missing since three o'clock this afternoon.' Surprise showed on her face. 'Hadn't you heard?' he said. 'I thought news got round quickly in Asshe.'

'We don't have anything to do with the Haffertys,' she said. She added something to the effect that they and her parents had been friendly, but they weren't any more. 'What do you think has happened to him? An accident?'

'He could have gone off without telling anyone, but we have to look, just in case,' he said. 'We'll have to look again soon as daylight comes.' He saw her shiver. 'Anyway what are you doing out at this hour?'

She hesitated, then she said slowly: 'I — that is, I thought I might meet you before you went back. I wanted to know what was going on. I saw you, and Charles Hafferty.'

'How did you spot it was us?'

'Field-glasses.' He hadn't noticed that she was using field-glasses. 'I get so bored,' she said. 'I have to amuse myself somehow.'

'Better not let anyone catch you at it, they might think you were spying on loving couples.'

He said it jokingly but he felt vaguely disturbed by her explanation. She stood there eyeing him coolly. 'Have a cigarette?' She took out a packet from her skirt pocket. He shook his head. She lit a cigarette for herself. She drew in the smoke and expelled it as if she was trying to exhale all her uncertainty on the cold night air.

'If you want to push on,' she said, 'don't mind me.'

He was conscious of a new closeness between them, and his tiredness might never have been. Perhaps it was the intimacy of the night, the loneliness of the road that seemed to bring them together. 'I suppose you'll have to be up frightfully early in the morning?'

He grinned. 'Frightfully.' Then he said: 'I'm a bit worried about you, being out like this, I mean.'

'You think I'll get hit over the head by a gipsy?'

'You never know who's around,' he said.

'If that was all I had to worry about — ' She broke off and looked away, as if she had blurted out something she had not meant to say. He stood looking at her. She put a hand lightly on his arm and then let it drop uncertainly. 'I like your dog,' she said. 'What's his name?'

'Hero,' he said. 'If there's anything I can do to help you, I wish you'd tell me.'

He felt separated from her, he thought, although it seemed irrational, only by the barrier of his uniform. He wondered how he could contrive to meet her in his ordinary clothes. She hadn't mentioned the girl. Perhaps she hadn't seen her; she had come out in the hope of speaking to him about what had been happening in Asshe Woods. She was bored, she had explained. Any excuse was a good excuse if it gave her something new to think about.

She gave a little nervous laugh. 'I suppose you think I'm spoilt, living at home and having everything done for me?'

'You're very young,' he said.

'I'm not so young,' she said, as he expected she would. 'Soon as I'm nineteen my parents have promised I can go and live in London.' He had thought she was older than she said. Nearer twenty, he would have said. 'The only thing is,' she went on, 'I don't know what I want to do. What job I can take on.'

'Why not be a policewoman?' he grinned at her.

But she did not smile back. They stood silently while a vast, dark cloud drifted across the sky and blotted out the moon. An owl screeched somewhere and another across the road answered it. Hero gave a tremendous yawn, and they both laughed. The moon emerged again and shone whitely over the trees.

'I think you ought to get some shut-eye,' P.C. Jarrett said.

'You have a long walk,' Fay Kelly said. She looked at the dog. 'Both of you.'

They walked back to Roselands together in silence. He opened the gate for her, and watched her go quickly and quietly to the front-door. She went on tip-toe. She opened the door, and he saw the glow of a light within. She turned and waved. The door closed on her.

He reached Professor Kane's bungalow. The exhilaration sparked by his meeting with Fay Kelly was fading. He was yawning his head off now, he felt all in. He had quite a distance to walk, and as he gathered his tired muscles to quicken his pace, a voice spoke to him out of the darkness.

'Good night, Mr. Jarrett.'

He halted, turned on his heel and snapped on his electric-torch. The circle of light framed Dr. Morelle as he stood by the gate to The Nest. He was smoking a cigarette, and its aroma came to P.C. Jarrett; it was an unusual tobacco-scent, intriguing. Egyptian tobacco, Jarrett decided. The tall, lean figure did not move, while the policeman noticed that Hero showed no sign of aggressiveness as might have been expected at the sudden voice, or sight of the stranger in the shadows.

'Dr. Morelle.'

Jarrett moved towards him.

'I was taking a breath of midnight air. It is more refreshing and conducive to sleep here than in Harley Street.'

'I'm sorry if you suffer from insomnia, Dr. Morelle.'

'It is merely that my brain is tangling with a problem which has been concerning me this past few days, so naturally it keeps me wide-awake. I shall sleep soundly when I go to bed in a quarter-of-an-hour.'

'That's all right, then.'

'Whereas you will still be trying to solve your difficulties when you are in bed; I prefer to put them aside the moment my head touches the pillow.'

'I'm afraid I often do work out things when I'm trying to get off to sleep.'

Dr. Morelle nodded understandingly, a spiral of cigarette-smoke curled up from the glowing tip of his cigarette. He was wearing a dark overcoat draped over his shoulders like a cloak; the wind ruffled his hair, which seemed to gleam like a raven's wing.

Dr. Morelle mentioned that he had learned something of the story of Tod Hafferty's disappearance from what Professor Kane had told him. Without realizing it, Jarrett found himself launched into an account of what he knew about it; Dr. Morelle gave no impression of drawing him out, yet it was a question deftly put here, a quizzical silence there, which got the other talking.

Jarrett told Dr. Morelle of what he had seen between the old-time film-star and the girl in the railway-compartment, adding his speculations concerning the possibility that she was mixed up with his disappearance. His reluctance to see her and question her, because he said, he felt he had to shield Tod Hafferty from the scandal and worse, if his association with the girl was made public.

He added how he had passed her not long ago, when she had been proceeding in the direction of Asshe House. Jarrett even found himself describing his meeting a few minutes back with Fay Kelly; there was little, as he talked quickly and vividly, that by the time he had finished Dr. Morelle didn't know about Tod Hafferty, his family, and his background.

There was a silence when he came to the end of it, Dr. Morelle offered no comment. An owl hooted and another answered it again from a distance.

'It's funny the way I've told you all this,' Jarrett said. 'I suppose it's pretty dull stuff to you.'

'Nothing which teaches us what makes human beings tick is ever dull.'

It was then that Jarrett remembered something.

'Dr. Morelle,' he said slowly, 'how was it that when you stopped your car earlier tonight, you knew that I was on the look-out for a man who was lost?'

Dr. Morelle took a deep drag at his Le Sphinx. P.C. Jarrett thought he detected the shadow of a smile at the corners of his mouth. 'If you expect me to blind you with an example of the science of rationcination,' he said, 'you are in for a disappointment. You inferred that you were searching for someone when you expressed your anxiety that I should not lose my way here.' Jarrett recalled what he had said when he had stopped the Duesenberg. 'That the missing person was a man seemed a reasonable assumption, since it is a matter of statistical record that more men disappear than women. The more cynically-minded assert that it is women that men disappear from.'

'I see.'

'I am gratified to have been able to enlighten you.'

One part of the other's brain was

deciding that he would phone Sandwich police-station as soon as he got back to Eastmarsh; a sudden sense of urgency had taken possession of him. As if Dr. Morelle's materialization out of the night came as some sinister warning to him that he must make every speedy effort to find the missing man. He hoped the poor old devil wasn't lying out in the wet grass somewhere. Stiff as a board he'd be when they found him.

Dr. Morelle had turned towards the gate. Then over his shoulder, he said, so quietly that the other only just caught the words: 'You may also be interested to know that something like eighty per cent missing persons return home of their own volition; almost ninety-nine per cent are eventually located.'

P.C. Frank Jarrett could feel his mouth open as he listened to this coolly offered example of Dr. Morelle's omniscience. The tall, dark figure seemed to melt into the darkness as the gate creaked open.

Then to Jarrett's ears came: 'By the way, only one case in three thousand proves to be murder.'

8

Marie Hafferty woke instantly, on the dot of 6.30 and at once she was fully alert. No lying in a half-waking dream for her; one moment sleep, the next full wakefulness. Not like her husband, Charles. It took an alarm-clock ringing away for several moments to bring him up from the depths of sleep. She had often wondered why his sleep habitually seemed to be one of such utter exhaustion, almost like that of an overworked manual-labourer.

She got out of bed and began to dress, choosing her clothes with more care than usual. Normally it was a pair of slacks and a jersey, but now she searched out a neat pencil-skirt, struggled into a girdle and sheerest stockings. From a drawer she took her newest, tight, figure-hugging sweater. Then went downstairs.

She gave a brief thought to her husband at Asshe House; had there been any news about his father? As she stood in the warm kitchen making a pot of tea, her mind revolved round Tod Hafferty. They would be sure to find him today. Last night the darkness had conspired against the searchers, but today it would be different. She considered her father-in-law and her thoughts were not over-generous.

She heard a sound upstairs and her head tipped back sharply, listening. So Nicky was in. He must have got back very late. She had waited up for him until nearly midnight.

Marie poured hot water into the teapot, stirred, then put the lid on. She laid out two cups, sugared them generously, poured milk into them then stood waiting while the tea matured in the pot.

Nicky Hafferty had found it impossible to live under the same roof as his father. Spoilt by his mother, and reckless, with no firm ideas about a career, he had tackled all sorts of jobs locally these past two years. A petrol-pump attendant; on the staff of a holiday-camp; working at a racing-car enthusiast's garage; job after job, all different and each one packed up within a short time. The last few months he had come to live at Woodview. The rows at Asshe House had become unbearable, Marie knew, and he paid her husband adequately for his keep and a roof over his head. Even a quid or two coming in each week was useful. Charles Hafferty was not a raging success as a commercial artist.

No telling how Nicky would take it, Marie was thinking. No love lost between him and Tod, of course; but this was a serious matter.

If only she could persuade her husband to work in London, Marie Hafferty mused, as she poured the tea and put the cups on a tray. Get himself a proper studio and really get weaving. She went upstairs noiselessly and put the tray on the chest of drawers which stood on the landing. Then she knocked on the door of Nicky's room and without waiting for an answer went in.

He lay sprawled half in, half out of bed, face down, arms flung wide. His eyes were closed but she knew he was not asleep. She put the cup of tea on the table at the bed-head. Then she stooped and touched the thick, blond hair.

'Nicky.'

He gave a groan and rolled over on to his back and looked up at her with his long-lashed, smoky-hazel eyes. He noted her unusual smartness and said vaguely: 'What's up?'

She sat on the side of his bed. 'You'd better listen to me,' she said. 'I've got a piece of news you won't like.'

At once his face went sullen; his thick eyebrows came down in a heavy frown. 'If it's bad news you can keep it to yourself,' he said. 'I've had enough to last me a month.' He heaved himself up on to his elbow.

'You know then?'

Nick Hafferty looked at her cautiously. 'Know what? Look here you'd better come out with it. Who's trying to nail me?'

She smiled and ran her forefinger lightly up his tanned bare arm. Obviously, he didn't know what had happened. 'It's Tod,' she said. 'He disappeared yesterday afternoon and nobody knows what's happened to him.'

He gaped at her, then he gave an abrupt snort of laughter. He broke off abruptly, and reached for the cup of tea. After he'd swallowed a mouthful, he said: 'That's a joke. What do they think he's done? Gone off with a piece?'

'No one knows what's happened to him,' she said carefully. 'Not even the local cop.'

'The police.' He slopped half his tea into the saucer, as he jerked a look at her. 'What in hell have they got to do with it?'

'Charles called them in yesterday afternoon,' she said. 'When he hadn't got back by tea-time, P.C. Jarrett from Eastmarsh came over. Later, they went out looking for him.'

'But they didn't find him?'

She shook her head. 'They'll be going out again this morning. If you want to join the search-party you'd better get up and get dressed.'

Her finger traced a path down over his shoulder. Then her fingers suddenly flexed and she dug her nails into his skin. Nicky's pyjama jacket was unbuttoned, showing his thick chest; he was quite unconscious of her, scowling at his own thoughts.

'I've got a filthy headache,' he said.

'Where did you go to, last night?'

She moved her hand and began to caress his arm. He had been making inquiries about a new job at the local golf-course, he said. But he hadn't come back when she went to bed, she said. He looked at her quickly. 'I just stayed out.'

'All right, if that's how you feel about it.'

'That's how I feel about it.'

She moved closer to him until her breasts inside the tight sweater were pressing against him. 'Charles will be wondering why you haven't gone down to Asshe House.'

'He doesn't need me. There's Alf Layton and your local copper, Jarrett.'

'I think you ought to go; it's your own father who's missing.'

'I suppose you're right,' he said, unwillingly. For the first time he seemed to become aware of her nearness to him. 'Clear out, will you, so I can get dressed?'

'It doesn't bother me,' she said.

He threw her a quick glance then he grinned and rolled out of bed. 'Please yourself.' He pulled off his pyjama coat and began hunting for his clothes. 'Haven't time for a bath,' he muttered. She picked up his shirt, and he put out his hand.

'Put your head down,' she said. As she slipped the shirt over his head he groped his arms into the sleeves. He stopped dead as he felt her hands encircle him.

'Stop it, Marie.'

She pressed herself against him. 'Why didn't you come home last night,' she whispered. 'I waited and waited. It was a perfect chance.'

'You're out of your tiny mind.' He gripped her wrists and threw her off. 'If you go on like this I'll move out, I swear I will.'

'No, you mustn't,' she said urgently. 'Please don't Nicky.'

'Behave yourself then,' he growled. He grabbed up his other clothes and half ran out of the bedroom. 'I'll get dressed in the bathroom,' he shouted back at her.

Marie stood in the empty bedroom, biting her lips. She went over to the window and looked out across the garden. Frost sparkled on the grass. It was barely full daylight, too early yet to know what the day would be like. She thought of the day ahead and caught her breath in a long sigh of boredom.

She hated everything that her life contained, the house, the little straggle of other houses that made Asshe; parochial interests of the local people. Her husband pottering about unsuccessful in his studio at the back of the house. There was nothing she could do except pick out of each day any scrap of excitement she could find, making situations simply for the thrill of handling them.

Charles knew she was bored, that was why he treated her so carefully. She grinned, knowing his fear of emotional scenes. He thought if he pretended the situation didn't exist it would never come to the boil. Well, he had a surprise coming. One of these days he would wake up and find her gone.

Abruptly she moved away from the window. She went down to the kitchen and found Nicky pouring himself more tea. He looked up as she came in. 'Do you want any breakfast?' she said.

'No. I'd better get going.' He struggled into a worn, leather coat, gulped off his tea, then slammed out without a word.

Marie watched him from the window. He looked lithe and powerful when he moved. She wondered where he'd been last night. Who with. She cooked herself breakfast.

Half-an-hour later found her on her way to Asshe House. The sun was up now and the sky was bright, a cold and clear blue-green. When she got to the house she saw P.C. Jarrett's bicycle propped against the gate. Her spirits lifted and she was suddenly glad she had dressed smartly. Then the front-door opened and they were all there, Charles, Nicky, Alf Layton and Jarrett.

If her husband noticed her unusual smartness he mentioned nothing about it. 'Glad you're here,' he said. He said it as if he meant it; as if he felt he could turn to her in this time of need. It made no impression on her. 'Mother's still asleep,' he went on. 'I saw she took something to make her sleep and she hasn't come out of it yet.'

Marie's thoughts went to Olivia and Bill Parker. Where were they? Olivia should be here, looking after her mother. As if reading her thoughts, Charles said: 'Olivia was over earlier. Then she went back to get Bill his breakfast.'

Marie shrugged and watched her husband and the others march off into the orchard.

No one talked. Even Alf Layton had nothing to say. P.C. Jarrett after a wakeful night, experienced the sense of unreality that follows on the heels of insomnia.

He had put the Sandwich lot in the picture; he had been told to go ahead with his own search as he had planned for daylight. They would circulate a description further afield, in case the missing man had left the locality. Jarrett had said nothing about Tod Hafferty and the girl. Sandwich had sounded as if he would turn up safe and with some excuse for his absence.

He breathed in the air to the bottom of his lungs. His eyes were heavy, and the rows of trees with the melting frost dripping from their branches looked like the backcloth of a dream. He heard Nicky Hafferty question his brother in a low voice, he was asking him the time yesterday afternoon when anyone had started to worry about Tod Hafferty's disappearance. It was a question which Nicky had asked before. As the other gave him the approximate answer, Jarrett wondered how much Nicky knew about his father's mode of life.

'We'll have to comb the woods from end to end,' Jarrett said to Alf Layton, close beside him. He turned to Charles Hafferty. 'You and I might try round the chalk-pit again, to start with.'

When they reached Asshe Woods, Nicky and Alf went off searching the undergrowth, while Jarrett and Charles Hafferty headed towards the chalk-pit, thrusting aside the brambles that tore at their clothes. They could hear Alf and Nicky behind them, going deeper into the woods. Jarrett wished he could have had Hero with him, but the scent was too cold, he felt sure.

He picked his way over the trailing wire that had once barred the path to the chalk-pit. He blinked dazzled eyes in the sunshine, wishing he felt less woolly-headed. He had lain awake half the night, his mind refusing to slow down. All sorts of pictures had chased round his brain. Meeting the girl so late; then meeting Fay Kelly; and there had been his talk with Dr. Morelle.

He stood now on the edge of the chalk-pit. He began to move slowly round, in places the side fell steeply away where the earth had crumbled. He heard Charles Hafferty crashing about in the bushes, and far away he heard his young brother as Alf Layton called out to him, shout back a laughing reply.

Then Jarrett stopped. He looked down over the chaos of rusted empty cans, over the holed buckets, worn tyres, tangled wire.

Tod Hafferty lay there, his head covered in blood.

9

At about the same time that Marie Hafferty had taken extra care in her choice of clothes that morning with her brother-in-law in mind, Dr. Morelle was at the wheel of the yellow Duesenberg, heading along the west bank of the River Stour, in the direction of Richborough.

He had slept soundly when he had returned to the bungalow after his meeting with P.C. Jarrett; Professor Kane had already gone to bed. Miss Frayle had gone sleepily to her room very shortly after she had arrived with Dr. Morelle. The fresh air, added to the fatigue of the last-minute rush of work in connection with a Soho murder-case which was being investigated by Detective-Inspector Hood, had been too much for her; she had left Dr. Morelle and Professor Kane talking over their whisky-and-sodas to fall asleep the moment her head hit the pillow.

What had brought Dr. Morelle out so early this morning, leaving the bungalow sleeping soundly behind him, had been to do with Kane's description of the derelict harbour at Richborough, where the River Stour widened out to run into Pegwell Bay. It had sounded fascinating; and P.C. Jarrett's description later of the local terrain which he had given during his account of Tod Hafferty's disappearance had prompted Dr. Morelle to look the locality over.

Or perhaps it was some intuition or some prescience which took a hand in his decision to take the Duesenberg for an early morning spin. He entertained little belief in intuition. But he would have agreed that there was something about the Tod Hafferty business which had taken hold of his imagination. The image of the missing film-star was not easily dismissed from the mind.

The recurrent squalls whipping in from the direction of the Goodwin Sands slapped his car as he sped along the winding road. He had left the sandhills and Bloody Point behind him. Now the saltings ran out to sea, lonely and smoothly gleaming where the pools and creeks caught the pale light of the dawn. Here was where the great marshy waste had spread until it engulfed the old harbour of Richborough.

Against the fading darkness of the skyline he could see the ruins of the Roman castle which overlooked the hamlet of Richborough itself and the old port. Once the crumbling castle had been the focal point of forts and Roman supply-bases; and it was odd to think that, embedded so deeply in the earliest history of the land, the harbour had come to life during the two world wars.

Now his objective lay ahead. Dr. Morelle's eye was caught by the huge travelling cranes standing motionless and rusted, towering over the silt and the open waste where it began to meet the tide. He had slowed the car. The road was empty and he might have been the only living human being in the world.

There was the old harbour, whose foundations deep, deep beneath the silt had been laid long centuries ago. He stopped the car, having pulled into the side of the road, and got out. The wind whipped him, but it was not as chill as he had anticipated. He walked slowly until he found a pathway off the road. He made his way along it, scanning the scene of incredible desolation before him.

Broken jetties which came to a crippled stop; mile upon mile of twisted wire, thick with rust, straggling everywhere like some fantastic weed. Long, empty huts and low buildings of rotting wood, their windows and doors caved in, and wooden barges half-sunk in the mud; nearby was the remains of a train-ferry which had conveyed troops and armaments across to France, whose rusted steel ruins stood out of the waste like old teeth.

It was here, in the anxiety-filled 1930's that Jewish refugees from Germany had lived, before finding homes elsewhere; it was here, in the war Hitler later unleashed that some 20,000 troops camped after Dunkirk.

Dr. Morelle looked back along the way he had come. The road had been screened off in war-time, so that travellers could not view the activities of the war-busy port; here part of the famous Mulberry Harbour had been assembled. He turned and lit a cigarette, cupping the flame of his lighter against the wind. He went on to where the path widened out into rough sandy stubble.

He was passing one of the huts, when he thought he caught the sound of a cough. He paused and listened. A marsh-bird cried harshly; now the sky was changing from the reddish gold of the dawn to a clear, bright opal. There came the little cough again. Someone was inside the hut.

Dr. Morelle moved quietly to the doorway, where the door hung askew from one hinge. The hut was lighted by the window, all its panes missing, except where some jagged edges stuck from the frame, opposite the door. In the far corner, to his right, the girl sat in a heap of blankets, staring at him.

'Hello?' she said. 'I wasn't expecting you.'

From the description Jarrett had given him last night of the girl with Tod

Hafferty, Dr. Morelle knew this was her. Beside her was an overcoat upon which was spread several garishly-covered magazines. They were film-fan magazines, he saw, as he approached the girl. There was a twenty-packet of cigarettes and a box of matches. Against the wall behind her a man's bicycle was propped.

She caught his glance. 'Belongs to a boy-friend of mine.'

She gave him a look of calculated amusement from beneath thickly mascaraed eyelashes. She patted a place beside her invitingly. But he stood eyeing her, and with a shrug, she turned to the magazine she had been reading, cigarette drooping from a full lower-lip. The magazine showed a girl on the cover, luridly captioned: Hollywood's Latest Glamour Doll. He noticed several cigarette stubs, with their lipstick traces, scattered around her.

'Who are you?' she said, without looking up, and turning a page. He told her his name. She shot him a look. 'A flipping doc,' she said. 'What you doing in these parts of an early morn?'

'Come to that, what are you doing here?'

'This is my home from home,' she said. 'I often come here. But for Heaven's sake, do take the weight off of your feet. You make me feel small, like a kid, standing over me. I don't like feeling small.'

He sat down beside her and lit a fresh cigarette. Her eyes flicked from his thin gold cigarette-case to his face.

She ran a pointed pink tongue over her lower-lip. She stubbed out her cigarette, and grabbed her handbag and began rummaging in it for a mirror and lipstick. As she worked on her face, she said: 'I bet you didn't expect to find little me here.'

'Life's full of surprises,' he said.

'Pleasant ones, I hope?'

'In this instance, yes.'

Her sidelong glance was sly, suddenly wary. She pushed the mirror and lipstick back into the handbag. He produced his cigarette-case and she took a cigarette, examining it curiously. He lit it for her with his lighter. She took a long drag at it. 'Not bad,' she said, and took another steady pull at the Le Sphinx. 'You a posh doctor?'

'I work in Harley Street.'

'In London?' She indicated the film-magazines. 'You ever cure any film-stars?'

'Film-actors and film-actresses are sometimes among my patients,' he said.

'Honest? Who?' She moved closer to him, and a wave of cheap scent enveloped him.

She was wearing a low-cut blouse under a jacket, and she gave Dr. Morelle every opportunity to observe that P.C. Jarrett's description of her physical attributes was correct in its details. She was well-developed for her age. 'I know a film-star,' she was saying, and his gaze fixed her. 'Least he was. He's a bit past it now. But I like listening to him chuntering away about when he was starring in films.'

'What is his name? I may know him.'

Again that sidelong, sly glance. 'You don't,' she said, 'otherwise you'd know who I mean. We only got one film-star round these parts. Even if he is a has-been. He says it's this tee-vee that's ruined his career,' she added inconsequentially. 'But he was too old.' She looked at him. Her smile was suddenly frank and innocent. 'I like chatting to you,' she said.

'Don't let me stop you,' he said, through a cloud of cigarette-smoke.

'I mean, you don't look as if you'll try any funny business.'

'I think you may rely on that,' he said.

'Not that I might mind all that much,' she said coquettishly. 'You got what it takes, in a way. As a lover-boy, I mean. Even if you're not so young. Well, we're none of us that.'

Dr. Morelle restrained a slight wince. He made no reply, but glanced round the hut, with its floorboards rotting away, and the wind whistling through the broken windows.

The girl coughed a little over a cigarette. She made the most of it, knowing he was looking at her. 'You should give me something for it,' she said. 'You're a doctor. Where's that listening-thing you have, to hear how your heart's behaving, and if you've got T.B., or not?'

She began undoing the buttons of her blouse.

'You're wasting your time,' Dr. Morelle said. She looked at him. 'I didn't bring my stethoscope with me.' He went on to tell her that she should see her local doctor, if she was worried about her cough. He would decide what was wrong and treat her accordingly.

'Oh, I can't be bothered,' she said. She left her blouse-buttons undone deliberately, leaning forward whenever she could and watching him to observe the effect she was having on him.

The daylight was filling out the shadowy corners, as the last remnants of the night were elbowed from the sky by the new day. He glanced at his watch. It was 7.40. He heard the girl say: 'When I get married, I'm going to have a real home, nothing cheap and flashy. In one of these mags there's a whole lot of pictures of a star's home in Hollywood. This one, the bedroom's got curtains made from a kind of fluffy fur. And there are fourteen bedrooms, each got its own bathroom, too. All done up in black marble and silver and mirrors. And it's got an indoor swimming-pool and its own cinema, with leopard-skin covered seats.'

'Well,' Dr. Morelle said, 'there's no place like home; not like this one, anyway.'

'You're dead right,' she said humourlessly.

She chattered on, blithely unaware of the incongruity of their surroundings, talking her pipe-dreams out loud to him, with the same lack of humour, the deadly seriousness as if it could all reasonably be expected to happen; and he could feel only pity for her. When her chatter came to a stop, and he said that he thought it was about time he was moving along, she suddenly flung her arms round him, her mouth sought his hungrily.

'Stay with me,' she murmured. 'I mean, you can do what you like with me, only don't go.'

He freed himself from her clinging arms and her firm, curving young body pressing urgently into him, and he got to his feet. She moved so that there was a flash of white thigh above her stockings, and her too-tight rucked-up skirt, and then she was standing beside him, her eyes glowing, her teeth glistening beneath her full lips. Her unbuttoned blouse had slipped off one shoulder.

He took her hands in his, and bent and kissed her, gently, on the mouth. 'Save it for Tod Hafferty,' he said. The reaction in her eyes told him all he wanted to learn.

'So you did know, all the time?' Suddenly she tensed and pulled herself from him, to eye him sulkily. 'You wouldn't fool me, would you? I mean, you're not a copper?'

'I happened to see you in the vicinity of his home,' he said.

'What, last night?' she said quickly, with a smile of surprised interest. 'I never saw you.'

'I caught sight of you from the window of the place where I'm staying.'

'Oh, I see; I saw a cop hanging about.' That sly, sidelong glance at him from under her thick eyelashes. 'And because you saw me near old Tod Hafferty's house, you put two and two together?'

He gave her a nod. She stared at him

for a few moments, as if making up her mind. 'I'll believe you,' she said, 'though thousands wouldn't.' A pause, and then: 'We had a date yesterday afternoon; he was supposed to have met me for a quick cuddle in Asshe Woods. He didn't show up; so, later, I thought I might hang around outside his house, in the hope he'd see me. He goes to bed late.'

She shrugged. He said nothing as she glanced down at her bare shoulder and then moved close to him. 'Okay, Doc,' she said. 'You're on the level. Only, you see, I'm under age. If anyone found out about him and me, there'd be trouble for the silly old chump. That's why I was scared you might be a cop.'

A brief paroxysm of coughing shook her.

He repressed a spontaneous move to hold her to him in a quick upsurge of sympathy. Instead he watched her, his eyes slitted behind the puff of smoke from his cigarette drooping from the corner of his mouth.

'You're certainly no woman-mauler,' she said breathlessly, when her coughing had stopped. 'Old Tod, he'd have had me undressed by now, all out of sympathy, of course.' Now her look was level and warm. 'You want to know something?' she said. 'It wasn't only because of him I was hanging about there, last night.'

He took the Le Sphinx from his mouth and made a step towards her.

'I better tell you,' she said.

About twenty minutes later Dr. Morelle was making his way back across the wasteland. He heard her cough and he turned back and saw her in the doorway. She waved to him, and then she was gone.

He reached the Duesenberg, and stood there for a moment, looking at the rusted, towering cranes, the ruined jetties and the interminable twisted wire; he turned his gaze from the derelict barges deep in the silt, to the ruins of the old castle, gleaming where a splash of cold sunlight caught them.

Dr. Morelle got into the car and reversing, headed back the way he had come. He found that he had quite an appetite for breakfast.

10

P.C. Jarrett called out quietly. 'Mr. Hafferty, come here quick,' and something in his tone brought the other running. They stood together staring down at the huddled body. Charles Hafferty had gone a deathly white.

'It's Tod,' he said, and started down the side of the chalk-pit.

We ought to have a rope, Jarrett thought, then he went down after the other, slipping and stumbling. The rusted cans slithered away under their feet; Jarrett lost his footing and saved himself by grabbing at an over-hanging bush. His heart lurched; Charles Hafferty looked back at him, and Jarrett called out that he was all right. He let go of the bush and slithered down to where the other stood.

The body was halfway down the side of the chalk-pit, lying on a shelf about four feet wide. Below it the side of the chalk-face fell away again about thirty feet to the bottom.

Jarrett called out quickly: 'Don't touch him.' Charles Hafferty stood waiting until the policeman joined him.

The sprawled figure's clothes were soaked, and frost still clung to the shoes which were screened from the morning sunlight by the overhanging side of the chalk-face. The body lay face downwards, left arm underneath, right arm limply stretched so that it hung partly over the edge of the shelf.

At the base of his skull was a big, messy wound. It had bled a good deal and blood was spattered all over the man's coat collar. There were blood-stains on the grass, Jarrett noted, though they were already hard to see, the dew and frost had faded them.

I'll have to touch him, find out if he's dead, Frank Jarrett thought. He struggled with overwhelming nausea, then remembered the old police joke, your first corpse is your worst. This is mine, he thought. This man's father, and he looked at Charles Hafferty. Can't be callous about it to help myself over the moment. First-aid training came back to him, the grinning, prostrate colleague undergoing artificial respiration, bandaging.

He reached out and took Tod Hafferty's wrist in a firm grasp. He felt for the pulse. Then he shook his head.

'He's dead,' Charles Hafferty said. 'I know that.'

'Been dead several hours, by the look of it.'

'You mean, he's been here all night?'

'Look at his clothes. Soaked. And there's frost on his shoes, hasn't had time to melt yet.'

'You think he fell over the edge?'

Jarrett was not listening. He stood up and regarded the body. Fix it all in your mind, he told himself. Everything you've seen, anything, however small, you've noticed; what anyone has said, at Asshe House, everything you've heard. Don't forget any of it. The other asked him the question again.

'He could have fallen,' Jarrett said. 'But would you get to a phone, quick as you can, and ring Sandwich police-station?

Tell them what we've found and ask them to come running. Yes, doctor, photographer, C.I.D. It's just routine,' he added hastily, seeing Charles Hafferty's face darken. 'They have to take a hand in a case like this.'

'What about you?'

'I'm staying. Don't want the others trampling about down here. Alf Layton is dim enough to try and move the body. Or your brother might.'

'You think he's been done in, don't you?'

P.C. Jarrett shifted uneasily. It looked damned suspicious, no doubt about it. He swallowed noisily. 'I don't know how he died, and until I do, I'm saying nothing. But if you want to help us find out, Mr. Hafferty, would you get on the phone for me, quick as you can?'

Charles Hafferty turned and began the scramble back to the top of the chalk-pit. By the time he finally made it, sweating, and over fifteen minutes had passed, there was no sign of Alf or Nicky. He went through the orchard at a shambling run. His head was a jumble of confused thoughts. How would he tell his mother? It would finish her. Tod had been her whole life ever since he could remember. For Helen Hafferty he had been all men rolled into one.

He heard Bess in the kitchen as he went into the house, the inevitable radio playing. Maybe his mother wasn't up yet. Maybe Marie had taken her breakfast up to her.

His mouth was dry and his heart thumped in his eardrums as he picked up the telephone. The desk-sergeant at Sandwich police-station took down the facts disinterestedly. Charles Hafferty described the shortest route to Asshe Woods and the man at the other end asked him, where was P.C. Jarrett?

'He stayed up there. Didn't want anyone trampling about until you'd come.'

'We'll be along as soon as we can.'

Charles Hafferty's hand was shaking as he put down the telephone. He caught a movement out of the tail of his eye, and spun round to see his wife at the foot of the stairs. She had come down so quietly, he had not heard her. Her face was blank but he knew she'd overheard everything.

'We found him halfway down the chalk-pit.' She looked at him silently. 'Damn great hole in the back of his head,' he said.

She found her voice. 'An accident?' she said in a rasping whisper.

Then he heard himself say as if he couldn't stop himself: 'Looks to me as if he was hit with a heavy stick.'

'The way you kill a rat,' she said.

He stared at her, his mouth a little open, like a child's. Then he shrugged and turned away, muttering over his shoulder: 'Where's Mother? She'll have to be told.'

'She's in bed; I've been up to see her a couple of times. She's got some tea and toast. Still a bit dopey from the sleeping-draught.'

'How do I break this to her?'

'I can't help you to do that,' Marie Hafferty said.

He gave a long, shuddering sigh, and went to push past her. Instead of standing aside, she stood her ground and he took her by the shoulders to shove her away.

118

She went tense under his grip and her eyes widened. He eyed her blankly, then thrust her away and went on heavily upstairs.

Marie put her hand to her mouth and bit fiercely on it, puncturing the skin with her sharp teeth. How stupid can a man be? What had happened to Charles? He hadn't always been like this. There were other men. She thought of Nicky, of Frank Jarrett. She supposed he was at the chalk-pit. If she was to make some tea and put it in a flask, it would give her an excuse to go out and see him.

She started for the kitchen to speak to Bess, before her husband came down. He'd stop her, find some job she ought to be doing. At that moment Alf Layton and Nicky appeared at the front-door and shouldered their way in. 'Tod's dead,' Nicky said loudly; 'lying in the chalk-pit. Been there all night, it looks like.'

'I know,' she said. 'Charles has just told me.'

'Damned cop won't let us near,' Nicky said. She saw that Alf Layton looked a bit green about the gills. Worse than Nicky. It

119

must have been a bit of a shock for them. 'I can't believe it,' Nicky went on hoarsely. 'I can't believe it's true.'

'It's true all right,' Alf said. 'That cop said so. He was stood by the edge of the chalk-pit, above where the body was.'

'Did Charles tell you he's got a head injury, a bad one?' Nicky said to Marie. She nodded, and he said: 'Where is Charles?'

'He's upstairs with your mother,' Marie said. She added: 'I wonder if she'll be the only one of us to shed any tears?'

'That's a charming thing to say,' Nicky flared.

'You're a charming family,' she said.

Alf Layton glanced from one to the other. 'Go on into the kitchen,' Nicky said to him. 'Tell Bess to make some tea.'

Alf crossed the hall slowly, his head sunken. Nicky swung round on Marie. 'What's got into you?' he said through his teeth.

'You can't make me believe you, for one, are sorry he's dead. All the things you've said about him.'

He came towards her, big and threatening. 'Shut your mouth,' he said in a low voice. 'Or I'll shut it for you.'

She shrugged and turned away towards the kitchen. Over her shoulder she threw at him: 'There'll be a lot of hypocrisy turned on today. Like some damned tap.'

He stood staring at her, his expression dark. Then he went upstairs.

P.C. Jarrett was standing quite still, his back towards her, when Marie saw him from the path to the chalk-pit. He looked very young, she thought. No more than 22, by the look of him. Fresh-faced and sincere. What would he be like off-duty? Probably he'd take up with some silly little piece instead of a woman who could teach him something about life. And then he'd never think beyond promotion to sergeant and getting his kids through the eleven-plus examination.

She eyed him coolly as she drew near. He was tall and well-built. Even in his police overcoat and helmet, he had an attractive air about him. She saw at once that he was not pleased when he caught sight of her. She called to him: 'I thought you might be cold, so I brought you some tea.'

She waved the thermos she had got Bess to fill. Bess had hardly known what she was up to, the shock of the news of Tod Hafferty's death had upset her so. Alf Layton had blabbed it all to her the moment he had got into the kitchen. It was the first time Marie had known the radio not to be turned on.

Jarrett took the thermos, muttering his thanks awkwardly. She guessed he was wishing she hadn't shown up. She watched while he unscrewed the cap and drank the steaming tea. She told him she hoped he had a sweet tooth, she had put sugar in. He said it was fine. Once or twice his gaze flicked across to her but he quickly looked away.

'You've found poor Tod Hafferty, then?' she asked.

He nodded. 'Did your husband telephone? I asked him to.'

'I heard him phoning,' she said. 'I think more police are on their way.' She saw the way he stood, barring her approach to the chalk-pit edge. 'Did someone do it?'

His face took on a wooden look. 'That's not for me to say. It could have been caused by falling over the edge in the dark. It should be properly fenced in.'

'He knew every inch of the woods and all around,' she said softly. 'And it was daylight when he went out for his walk. He'd no more fall down there than I would.'

'We must wait for the reports,' he said stolidly. He tried not to sound pompous. But he had to keep her at arm's length. He poured some tea, spilling it in his embarrassment.

She watched him as he drank. 'Supposing it wasn't accidental death?' she said. 'There'll be detectives around here, won't there? Questions asked?'

He eyed her over the thermos-cap. 'What are you getting at?'

She smiled what she imagined was one of her secret smiles. 'Only if there's ever anything you want to know that you think I might be able to help you about, don't forget to ask.'

He struggled with the distaste he felt for her. It occurred to him, she might be useful, if there was any trouble. She had sharp eyes and picked up gossip, he calculated. It was his job as a police-officer to ingratiate himself with people who kept their ear to the ground. He thought it likely that she would know as much as anyone about the dead man's amorous inclinations. If not more; and he had a shrewd idea that if he played his cards right she would talk to him.

He followed the direction of her glance. She was looking across to where the Kellys' house lay within its walled garden.

'I wonder if they'll have a bit of a shock when they know,' she said.

He knew that Major Kelly was a retired army type, while his wife was always elegantly dressed. He recalled that from what Fay Kelly had said last night that her parents had been on friendly terms with the Haffertys; then, he supposed, something had happened, some quarrel, and they had stopped seeing so much of each other. He said sharply: 'Why?'

She raised her eyebrows at the snarl in his tone. She wondered what he knew that had caused it. 'No particular reason,' she said idly.

He knew she was lying. He tucked her words away to be considered later, while his own gaze went back to the house. What could the Kellys know about Tod Hafferty, alive or dead, that the news about him would shock them all that much? That was what her tone hinted.

Her voice interrupted the questions which darkened his face.

'Look.'

He followed her outflung hand to where the two black police-cars approaching along the road from Sandwich, were slowing as they neared Asshe House.

11

At her bedroom-window Fay Kelly was focusing her father's army field-glasses on Marie Hafferty and P.C. Frank Jarrett. The powerful lenses had brought them so close she could make out their expressions; she felt she could almost hear what they were saying to each other. She had seen the woman's arrival with the thermos-flask, and had experienced an oddly jealous pang as she watched Frank Jarrett drink the tea. She wished she had thought of taking some out to him.

But she wasn't dressed; she was in her dressing-gown idly wondering what sort of day it was going to be when she had caught sight of the dark blue, helmeted figure in the distance, where she knew there was the old, disused chalk-pit. A secret kind of excitement had urged her to find the field-glasses and get a better view of P.C. Jarrett on duty.

Now, Marie Hafferty pointed to something out of Fay's line of vision, and Jarrett handed back the flask to her. They exchanged a few more words and then she hurried off, while the dark blue figure waited, staring in the direction Marie Hafferty had pointed.

Fay Kelly presumed it was all something to do with Tod Hafferty's disappearance yesterday; perhaps he had been found. Perhaps they had seen a car which was bringing him back to Asshe House? In that case, it occurred to her, why did Frank Jarrett remain where he was, a lonely sentinel? What was he guarding?

She gave up puzzling it out, instead her thoughts centred on Jarrett himself. She wondered what he would think of her if he knew about Nicky Hafferty.

Guilt and shame struggled within her as she remembered that meeting with Nicky. Excitement too, a sheer physical trembling. How long would it go on, this state of uncertainty? How old did you have to be before you woke up and knew what you wanted, knew what sort of a person you were? Now, at eighteen, she seemed to be half a dozen different people. She had not found her own identity.

Only the face in the mirror was constant, a pretty face with dark serious eyes and a sensuous mouth. Suppose the body wanted one thing and the mind another? What was the answer then? Gratify first one, then the other? Or hold back in the hope of finding someone when both could be satisfied? Suppose that never happened? Surely it was better to try things, find out if they were what you wanted, then be strong enough to reject them and try again?

Things, she told herself bitterly. No, not things. Men. That was what it came down to. She had wanted Nicky, and yesterday he had taken her.

She shivered emptily, remembering it. No one must ever know about that.

Into her line of vision she saw half-a-dozen men moving quickly in the direction of the chalk-pit. Some were in police uniform, some in plain-clothes. Jarrett remained where he was; he did not come forward to meet them. They must have found Tod Hafferty, she thought. What had happened? Was he dead? Fay thought about her mother. How would she take the news?

Her thoughts doubled back on what she had overheard several nights ago, between her father and mother. They had been quarrelling, raising their voices, and she could not help listening outside the sitting-room door.

'What you care about most is the blow to your own ego,' she had heard her mother tell her father. 'Because he's older than you, you're shattered that I find him attractive. Let me tell you he's a damn sight more of a man than you are.'

Fay had realized she was talking about Tod Hafferty; it explained the strange atmosphere which for some months now had seeped into the friendship between her parents and the Haffertys, so that her own meetings with Nicky had to be kept on an underhand basis. Fay had felt no sense of shock; she knew her mother had been unfaithful before, she had known it when she was barely in her teens. All she felt was pity for her father.

'But, if it's any consolation to you,' her mother had continued, 'it's finished, by mutual consent. I don't ever want to talk about it again. Not to you or anyone else. And if you're sweating in case the locals know about it, well you needn't. Nobody knows about it except Tod and me. And now you, as if you hadn't guessed before.'

She remembered wondering if her mother was lying, if she really had given up Tod Hafferty? Or had he given her up? And she was thinking how painful it had been to listen to her father's protests, his attempts to assert his dignity. It was as if he himself had always known he was ineffective, that all he had to offer his wife was his amiability and charm.

Now her thoughts switched to yesterday afternoon. She had met Nicky in Asshe Woods and he had asked her to marry him. She had refused. She had been unable to explain why, that it was because of what she knew about her mother and his father, and he had thought she had turned him down because he had no money, and no prospects. It was then she had let him make love to her.

Afterwards she had wept until her face was blotched and puffy, while Nicky, shamefaced and frightened, had tried to comfort her. She could not understand why she had allowed it to happen. He had asked her again to marry him, and again she had refused.

Fay Kelly turned away from the window and threw herself on her bed, full of a sudden agony in her heart as she tried to tell herself it was the first and last time. And yet she lay dry-eyed remembering the cold, misty magic of the woods and the feel of Nicky Hafferty's tweed jacket against her face.

Presently she returned to the window. The field-glasses showed her the movement of figures in the direction of the chalk-pit; the winking sunlight of the February morning glinted on something metallic, which looked to her like camera equipment. She had a quick bath and dressed. Breakfast would be ready at 9 a.m. It was a quarter to the hour. She hurried out of her bedroom and downstairs.

She saw her father in the garden and went out through the sitting-room french-windows. When he saw her, Major Kelly smiled, and his thin, anxious face lit up. 'Hello, Fay. You'll be cold without a coat. Quite nippy this morning.'

Despising your father, she had realized, a year ago, makes you grow up overnight. No matter how much she loved him, she had felt herself on a different footing with him. Nothing he could say would ever affect her very deeply again. She ignored his banal comments about the weather.

'Saw you at your window,' he went on. 'What had caught your eye?'

'Just watching the police,' she said, with affected carelessness. 'I suppose they have found Tod Hafferty.'

She clutched his arm as his face lost all its colour. 'The police?' He opened and closed his mouth, searching for words. 'But do you mean something's happened to him?'

She shrugged. 'Why pretend to be upset? He was a nasty old man, and if he's dead, so what?'

He stared at her, his small, weak mouth

still working beneath the typical clipped moustache. 'I must find your mother,' he said, after a few moments, 'It will be a shock.' Then he looked at her quickly. 'After all,' he said, by way of explanation for his reaction to her news, 'they are our neighbours.'

She turned away from him.

'I didn't even realize he was missing, exactly,' he said. 'I mean, this is all news to me.'

'I'm going into breakfast,' Fay said, unconcernedly over her shoulder. 'If you like, afterwards, I'll go and ask P.C. Jarrett what's going on.'

'My dear girl, I don't imagine the police have time to waste talking to you,' he said irritably.

'He will,' she said calmly. 'He's a friend of mine.'

'Well, he has no business to be,' her father said and looked at her uncertainly. Irrelevantly he added: 'Maybe we could have found a different place to live. I don't know. But there's nothing for us here. It must be rotten dull for you.' She made no reply. Her father said: 'If you do find out anything, will you let me know? I think I'll go up and see your mother, I don't feel much like breakfast. Bit of a shock, this business.'

Fay Kelly hurried out of the house after gulping down some breakfast. She came to where the two black, shiny cars were parked by the side of the road. The sun was bright and gave some warmth to the air; the wind was screened by Asshe Woods. She heard voices from the direction of the chalk-pit. Fay shivered involuntarily. No old man could fall down that horrible place and live.

She stood looking at the bustle and movement at the edge of the pit. A man was packing up his camera equipment. Others were searching the area, their heads moving from side to side, like automatons. There were two plain-clothes men in conversation. One stolid, middle-aged, had a typical policeman's face, she thought; anonymous features, sharp eyes. She saw Frank Jarrett come across and speak to the sharp-eyed man, who nodded.

Jarrett came towards her without at

first seeing her. When she moved forward to meet him, he glanced back at the two plain-clothes men, and she smiled. So he did not want to be seen talking to her, in business hours?

'Good morning,' he said to her, formally. 'What are you doing here?'

'I saw all this going on,' she said. 'They've found him, haven't they?'

'Yes. He was down the chalk-pit. Been there all night.'

'Dead?'

'Yes, very.'

She heard herself ask: 'An accident?'

He didn't answer.

She felt a little sick. 'You mean, somebody — ?'

She broke off as she saw that his eyes had shifted from her to beyond her shoulder. She turned quickly, to see the young woman wearing a dark beret slanted on her blonde head approaching. She wore horn-rimmed spectacles, behind which her blue eyes were wide and curious.

'Hello, Miss Frayle?' Fay Kelly heard Jarrett say.

'Good morning.' Miss Frayle smiled,

and then glanced at the girl. It was a warm, friendly smile.

Jarrett introduced them.

'Miss Frayle is staying with Dr. Morelle at Professor Kane's for the weekend.'

Fay Kelly murmured something to the effect that she'd met Professor Kane, and wasn't he a scientist or something like that? She added that she had, of course, heard of Dr. Morelle.

'It was supposed to be a quiet weekend,' Miss Frayle said. 'But there seems to be some excitement going on. Dr. Morelle was out at the crack of dawn, I know, though he wouldn't tell me what it was all in aid of.' Jarrett was watching her intently. 'He doesn't always tell me everything,' she said to him.

'There's been one development since last night, anyway,' he said. He gave a nod over his shoulder.

'You mean, about the man who disappeared?'

'Tod Hafferty,' the other said. 'They've found him down the chalk-pit. Dead.'

'More than dead,' the girl said. 'He's been murdered.'

Miss Frayle gave a little gasp. 'I'm sorry.' To the girl: 'Was — was he a friend of yours?'

'I knew him, not very well.'

'I didn't say he'd been murdered,' the policeman said, not very convincingly, Miss Frayle thought.

'You didn't have to say it,' Fay Kelly answered. 'It's in your face.'

Miss Frayle gave her a quizzical look from behind her horn-rims. Then she turned to regard the scene. The activity she was witnessing was the kind with which she was not altogether unfamiliar. She gave a little sigh. It seemed grotesque that sudden death should stalk this quiet little backwater.

Dr. Morelle had been anticipating a restful visit with Professor Kane, before returning to London to continue work on the Soho case. And she had been looking forward to some fresh air and one or two quiet walks, which was why she had brought her sensible low-heeled shoes. Professor Kane, she knew, was engaged on some mysterious research which Dr. Morelle wanted to discuss with him, and she had been hoping that his mind would be taken off crime and such sordid business.

Now, as she took in the obvious plainclothes types and the dark uniforms, she gave another, deeper sigh. Then she saw the girl's face, and she sensed something off-key about her, as if some deep apprehension held her in its grip. She spoke to her impulsively.

'I hope this hasn't upset you?'

Fay Kelly switched on a faint smile. 'It is a bit of a shock,' she said.

'If I can be of any help,' Miss Frayle said, then blushed a little shyly, afraid that she was butting in; 'I mean, I'm quite used to this sort of thing.'

Her voice trailed off, and the other's smile was less forced.

'You're very kind,' she murmured. 'I think,' turning to Jarrett, 'I'll be getting back. I — I don't quite know what made me come.'

Miss Frayle watched the girl hurry away, then she became aware of the figure of P.C. Jarrett next to her, and she turned to him and caught his expression as he also watched Fay Kelly. He was frowning, as if, Miss Frayle thought, her arrival on the scene had affected him in some way rather disturbing.

She started to make some conventional remark about the discovery of the dead man, when she gave a little gasp that drew the other's gaze to her.

'What is it, Miss Frayle?'

She smiled at him weakly. 'Nothing. I just thought of something — er — something I've forgotten to mention to Dr. Morelle.' She blushed as she always did whenever she had to tell a lie, however white it was. She gave a little gulp. 'You did say,' she went on, 'that his name was Hafferty? Tod Hafferty.'

Jarrett nodded. 'Used to be a famous film-star. Dead, now, all right. Down the chalk-pit.'

Tod Hafferty, she was thinking. That was the name in her dream, or nightmare, or whatever it was, at the dentist's on Friday. Tod Hafferty, the old-time film-star. That was who it was, she was sure. She had seen his name on the book Dr. Morelle had been reading in the train.

The Life and Loves of Tod Hafferty, she remembered the title clearly.

And now he was lying only a few yards from her, dead.

12

Nola Kelly called out to her daughter: 'Is that you, Fay?'

Fay had hoped to get up to her room unobserved. Now her mother would have to be told. She went slowly into the sitting-room. Sunshine sparkled in through the diamond window-panes, a bright fire burned in the brick hearth. The tall, slim woman turned from the fireplace as her daughter came into the room.

'Where have you been?' she said frowning. 'You promised you'd go over to Sandwich for me.'

'I'm sorry, I forgot.'

For a long time Fay had realized that her mother was jealous of her increasing prettiness and sophistication. Relations between them had been cool, with the increasing inevitability of a complete break. Only the presence of her anxiety not to cause her father any further unhappiness held her back from open quarrelling with her mother. There was the knowledge, too, that if the situation worsened she would have to leave home, and she had nowhere else to go to.

'There's something I ought to tell you,' Fay said.

'Oh?'

'About Tod Hafferty.'

Nola Kelly's hard, beautiful face tightened in anger.

'Hadn't you better learn to mind your own business?' she said quietly ominous. She moved towards Fay, her pale eyes set wide apart beneath a broad, smooth brow like chips of ice.

'You don't understand,' Fay said. 'I'm afraid there's bad news about him. Perhaps you know already; has Father told you?'

'He's out somewhere, he's said nothing to me. Nothing that made sense, anyway. But perhaps that was too much to hope for.'

Fay said woodenly: 'I'd better tell you then. There's been an accident. Tod Hafferty was missing all last evening, people went out searching for him.

They've just found him.'

The other stood perfectly still.

'What are you trying to tell me?'

'The chalk-pit. The police are there now, taking photographs and all the rest of it.'

'Where?' Nola Kelly frowned at her, uncomprehendingly.

'He was found in the chalk-pit, dead. I — I'm sorry, Mother.'

But as Fay made to go towards her impulsively as she swayed a little, her mother recovered herself with a tremendous effort. She turned and blundered across to the writing-desk, and picked up a long, silver box of cigarettes. She tried to get one out, but spilled a dozen which scattered all over the floor.

Unaware of it, she lit her cigarette from the lighter on the desk. 'I can't believe it,' she said in a low voice. 'How do you know all this?'

'It's true enough. I've just come from there.'

Her mother started to say something automatically about what was Fay doing out there, but the sentence died away. She

143

said: 'How did it happen?'

'I don't know.'

'How could he have fallen down there; Tod?'

'I don't think it was an accident.'

'What did you say?' the other asked harshly.

'I don't think it was an accident. I think — '

She broke off and they stood looking at each other. Fay thought how hard was her mother's reaction, how cold. He can't have meant much to her. She's not even upset.

'But if it wasn't an accident,' Nola Kelly said, then lapsed into silence, the sentence unfinished. She took a deep drag at her cigarette. 'It doesn't make sense. Who'd want to — ?'

Again she broke off and stared at her daughter coldly.

'I'm sorry,' Fay mumbled. She longed to rush away, to be alone, with her own thoughts. She wanted no part of her mother's sex-life. She did not want to be involved in it for a moment.

'I can't believe it,' the other was saying.

'You say your father knows?'

'He knows he's dead. I thought he came up to tell you.'

Nola Kelly nodded. 'I pretended to be asleep, I didn't want to talk to the fool. I haven't seen him since I came downstairs.' Her spoilt, beautifully made-up mouth curled. 'He hadn't the guts to tell me that. I had to find it out this way. From you. You may as well know — if you didn't already — that Tod and I were — '

'I thought he'd be waiting for me when I got back,' Fay cut in quickly. The longing to get away was overpowering. The familiar scent her mother used seemed suddenly overpowering, sickening. Tod Hafferty must have known that scent, she thought idly.

She went quickly to the door. 'I think I'll go and find Father.'

'Do that,' her mother said. 'He'll be interested to know all the details.'

Fay stared at her. She had taken the news of Tod Hafferty's death coolly, but now she was working herself into an unpleasant frame of mind over her husband. Fay shrugged and went out of the room.

She had no intention of looking for her father; all she wanted was to be alone in her own room. As she reached the hall to hurry upstairs, she saw out of the corner of her eye, the front-door start to open. She thought it was her father, and she made for the stairs.

'Fay.'

She turned, her heart thudding with panic. It was Nicky Hafferty who stood there. He came round the door quickly, shut it and stood with his back against it.

'I had to come,' he said.

He looked taller than ever and wide across the shoulders. His blond hair looked almost white, it was ruffled and boyishly untidy; his whole face was distraught.

'Go away,' she said. 'You must be mad to come here.'

He crossed to her, as she started up the stairs. 'I've got to talk to you. It's about Tod.'

She glanced around. Her mother or her father might appear at any moment. 'I know all about it,' she said. 'He's dead, and I'm sorry. But please go.'

'Don't you understand?' Nicky said desperately. 'They say Tod was killed yesterday afternoon, about three o'clock.'

'Well?'

'One of the cops has been to the house. I heard him talking to Charles. At about three o'clock, they think it happened.'

She stared at him wildly, only half-understanding the drift of his words. All she could see was that he was frightened about something.

'Don't you get it?' he said harshly, with his mouth forming a little line of impatience.

'I — I — ' She shook her head to clear her mind, but he misunderstood her.

'We — you and I — were in Asshe Woods at 3 p.m.,' he grated.

She gave a horrified gasp. The hall seemed to spin round her. Nicky came up the stairs to her. 'They'll ask questions,' he said in a low voice. 'We've got to think up a story. Find some reason for being in Asshe Woods.'

She could see he was scared stiff; and

now his fear had the effect of calming her.

'We can't talk here,' she said in a low voice.

She gave a look upstairs. She beckoned him and he followed her. When she reached her room and had shut and locked the door, he went across to the window and looked out.

'Don't let anyone see you,' she said quickly. He drew back, but didn't look at her. 'Nobody must know about yesterday afternoon,' she went on quietly. 'I'm pretty sure no one did see us there.'

He said unhappily: 'I don't know.'

'Where did you go after I left you?'

'I walked a hell of a long way,' he said sullenly. 'I can't remember exactly. I was wandering about for a long time. In the end I got down to the main road and there was a bus coming so I got on it. I spent the rest of the day in Sandwich.'

'What did you do there?'

'I don't know. Mooched around cafés and I had one or two drinks. Didn't get back till damned late.'

He turned and looked at her. He came at her from across the room and took her by the shoulders. A wave of pity for him swept over her. His grip tightened on her shoulders and gently she tried to free herself. He let her go.

'Who told you about Tod?' he asked her.

She hesitated before she answered him. He caught her reluctance to speak, and his eyes narrowed.

'I went to the chalk-pit just now,' she said. 'I'd been looking out.' She indicated the field-glasses lying on the table by the window. 'There was obviously something going on. Frank Jarrett told me.'

'The local cop? You sound as if you're quite pally.'

'He's quite nice,' she said. She made her voice sound as casual as she could; tried not to appear defensive. 'Does your mother know?'

He shook his head. 'Charles was trying to pluck up courage.'

Her thoughts went off at a tangent. She was wondering about her own mother and what would happen between her and her father. Would Tod Hafferty's death drive an even thicker wedge of hatred between them? It could have the opposite effect, she supposed. It could draw them together again. But somehow she didn't think so.

Suddenly Nicky's arms went round her, and she stiffened. Then as she had done that other time, she struggled, but his grip tightened.

'Don't fight me,' he whispered. His voice was thick, compelling. 'You know I love you.'

A terrible weakness assailed her. She lay inert on the bed where he had forced her as he began to smother her with kisses. She stared up past his blond head at the ceiling. She closed her eyes.

How could it be so different, she found herself reflecting hopelessly. Yesterday had been excitement, passion. This was nothing, just humiliating; and worse than that when he began saying how sorry he was, that he hadn't meant it.

She got off the bed calmly. Nicky tried to put his arms round her shoulders with a kind of clumsy tenderness that should have been touching. But it wasn't, not this time.

She was astonished by her objectivity; it was as if she was looking at two other people, as she rearranged her hair and saw both their reflections in the mirror. She heard herself insisting that no one must know about them, about yesterday afternoon, about this morning.

Why was she so anxious it should not come out? Because it was over and done with, she told herself. Ended as soon as it had begun. What had happened, to strip the excitement from it within the space of twenty-four hours? She had gone nowhere, seen no one.

Except Frank Jarrett, she thought. On the moonlit road, last night, and this morning. But that was ridiculous, she argued with herself. A village policeman? It wasn't that she felt any social distinction; it was just that it didn't add up with her dreams of a husband. She unlocked the door.

'I'll go first,' she said over her shoulder. 'I'll see if anyone is about.'

She turned to him, tried to appear affectionate.

He eyed her anxiously. 'And you think it'll be all right? I mean, about yesterday?'

She wondered idly if this second act of love-making had been motivated on his part by an attempt to make sure of her loyalty to him. It was an ungenerous thought and not very flattering, either. But he was obviously terrified that she would deny that he had been with her in Asshe Woods at 3 p.m.

She smiled at him. 'If the worst comes to the worst,' she said, 'I'll have to be your alibi, won't I?'

She thought she saw a relaxation of the tension that held him.

'I don't know,' he said.

'Not to worry; it may never happen.'

She went quickly downstairs, then stopped as she heard footsteps below. Nicky stood close behind her. It sounded like the daily help going to the kitchen. A door closed, and she went on down. The sitting-room door was open, but there was no sound of her mother in there. Fay felt certain she had gone upstairs again.

Nicky stayed close behind her as she went across the hall. Her heart was pounding away, but she felt clear-headed as she opened the door quietly and he slipped out. He turned as if to speak to her, but she gave him a quick smile and closed the door in his face.

She turned to go back to her bedroom, and then the reaction set in. She felt suddenly weak at the knees and longed to cry with self-disgust and the oppression of guilt. She must have been out of her mind, she told herself, biting her lip in an effort to keep back the tears.

There was a hurried movement above, a choking whisper which brought her head up. Her mother stood at the top of the stairs.

'What is it?' Fay went across the hall and began to go up the stairs.

Nola Kelly was gibbering. She couldn't form the words she wanted to say. She began to point, her slender, white hand jerking.

Fay dashed upstairs past her mother, and went along to the latter's bedroom. She occupied a separate bedroom. Fay looked in; everything seemed normal. She came out and saw her mother still at the head of the stairs but staring at her. She was gibbering away uncontrollably.

For a dreadful moment Fay thought she had gone suddenly insane. The slender white hand was still jerking at something beyond the bedroom. Fay looked over her shoulder. The bathroom door was wide open.

She moved towards it; the choking noise behind her reached a crescendo. Shakily, she reached the bathroom. It seemed oddly quiet, contrasting with her mother's inarticulate commotion. Fay went into the bathroom, her nostrils filled with the scent her mother used.

She stopped dead in her tracks, transfixed by the sight of the figure slumped over the bath.

13

Miss Frayle had stayed for a few brief words with P.C. Jarrett, who had been professionally non-committal, even though it was the famous Dr. Morelle's secretary, and then she had left, still preoccupied with the realization that the name of the man lying dead in the chalk-pit and the name she had seen while under the dentist's anæsthetic were the same.

She felt impelled to hurry back to The Nest where she knew Dr. Morelle was exchanging views and opinions with Professor Kane in his conservatory, that was also the laboratory, at the back of the bungalow.

Her thoughts, caught up as they had been by the rush of speculation concerning faded film-star Tod Hafferty, had been distracted temporarily by the sight of Fay Kelly disappearing in the direction of her home; there had been something about the girl which aroused her sympathy. Or was it more than sympathy? The question suddenly interposed itself between Miss Frayle's recollection of the girl's pale, tensed features. Added to which, Miss Frayle had sensed unerringly a subtle atmosphere between the other and the young policeman.

Miss Frayle was perfectly aware of that romantic side to her nature which was inclined to prompt her to perceive love blooming where in fact, no such thing was even in the bud; but all the same she had at once noted that the young policeman, P.C. Jarrett, was definitely attractive, and so was Fay Kelly. And, Miss Frayle knew, when two attractive people got together on the boy meets girl basis, romance was inevitably not far away.

But was there more to Fay Kelly's interest in what had transpired in the vicinity of the chalk-pit than the good-looking young policeman? Did the young woman's interest lie in something to do with Tod Hafferty? And now her mind swung back to tangle with the cause of her hurried return to Dr. Morelle. Her conjectures about Fay Kelly and her interest in the policeman or the death of Tod Hafferty, or both, gave place to considering the uncanny coincidence that tied up that which had entered her brain while in the dentist's chair with what she had recently learned at the chalk-pit.

It occurred to her that she might be wiser not to mention the matter at all to Dr. Morelle. Instinctively she slowed her pace as she proceeded along the road towards The Nest. The tap-tap of her sensible low-heeled shoes became less hurried, as she visualized the expression that could flicker across Dr. Morelle's saturnine features when she explained the coincidence to him. What importance would he give to a triviality which she had experienced while she was under the influence of an anæsthetic and something of deadly seriousness which had, in fact, taken place?

Miss Frayle began to baulk at the prospect of risking Dr. Morelle's sarcasm, and her thoughts went off at a tangent. Dr. Morelle had gone off in the Duesenberg before breakfast, she knew;

he had casually mentioned it to her on his return. She had asked him what had interested him to the extent of luring him out at such a relatively early hour that morning. Apparently, something that Professor Kane had said about the old, disused harbour over at nearby Richborough had taken his interest, and he had decided to view the scene.

And yet, Miss Frayle was recalling now, he had said little about it over breakfast, which he had eaten with a good appetite, which he had ascribed to the invigorating air of the saltings of Pegwell Bay. Even when Professor Kane had asked him one or two questions about it, his replies had been somewhat non-committal. This notwithstanding the fact that he had been intrigued enough in the first place to drive out there before breakfast.

Miss Frayle frowned to herself behind her horn-rimmed spectacles. Had Dr. Morelle in some way been made aware of the discovery of Tod Hafferty's body at the chalk-pit? Was his before-breakfast trip something to do with it?

If that was the case, then, what

contribution could she make to the sinister business? Dr. Morelle would certainly not want to hear her account of what had happened in Mr. Carlton's dentist's-chair. She gave a deep sigh, as her pace became less enthusiastic.

Why did Dr. Morelle always have to become involved in this sort of thing, she asked herself? It was a question which she had asked more than once in the past; and had never learned the answer. As if there wasn't enough sudden death and nasty goings-on in London to keep him busy, without finding it on the doorstep, down here, in this out-of-the-way spot, where he had come for a harmless weekend with an old friend.

A little while later found her back at the front-gate of The Nest, still undecided whether to give Dr. Morelle the dubious benefit of the coincidence of her dream-like or nightmarish, image of the name of the man who lay, grimly real, dead in the chalk-pit.

Miss Frayle paused as she opened the white swing-gate, and stared around her at the quiet scene. The road ran past

159

without anyone in sight. She glanced at her wrist-watch. It was approaching 10 a.m., and the lulling sense of a typically rural Sunday morning hung almost tangibly on the fresh, sunny air.

Miss Frayle glanced across the fields to her left, where Asshe Woods made a dark silhouette of intermingled skeletons against the sky, where the blueness mingled into the grey of the horizon. The police-activity that she knew was continuing was hidden from her now by a turn in the road, marked by a clump of tall bushes. From here she could see the roof-top of the house into which Fay Kelly must have gone, with its brick arch and high iron gates; and further on could be glimpsed a thin feather of smoke rising from another house, which she had passed. The name on the gate had been: Woodview.

She went inside the gate of The Nest and it swung to as the gravel of the wide drive crunched beneath her shoes. Now the road was almost completely masked by the tall trees on either side of the gate.

Miss Frayle went into the low-built,

brick bungalow and made her way through to the green-baize door which opened into the conservatory, off which ran the laboratory. She could hear Dr. Morelle and Professor Kane talking, the latter's voice raised animatedly in answer to Dr. Morelle's quietly incisive tones.

The conservatory looked out on to a small walled-in orchard of mixed fruit trees, some of which climbed the walls. Miss Frayle could hear sounds of Professor Kane's housekeeper moving about upstairs, as she debated whether she should or should not mention the Tod Hafferty coincidence to Dr. Morelle. She hadn't made up her mind as she stood in the open doorway leading to the laboratory itself and gave a little cough.

'Oh, Dr. Morelle,' she said.

His back was towards her, and he didn't, or preferred not to, hear her. But Professor Kane's deceptively plump face lighted up at her appearance at the door. His attempt to halt Dr. Morelle in the middle of what he was saying was ineffective, however. Dr. Morelle had suddenly decided to take over the conversation for his own, and was holding forth, as Miss Frayle grasped at once, on one of his favourite subjects.

'In the case of the paranoic,' he was saying, 'the wide world itself is distorted from the sane observer's view point, but from the patient's it assumes a mathematical logic all its own. You might say that he is a dreamer in reverse. Where you and I on awakening from a dream can recognize its illogicalities, which while we were dreaming seemed perfectly logical, the paranoic waking from a dream would recognize it as logical while the world into which he awoke would to him, be composed of the illogicalities of the dream.'

He was discussing almost the very subject she wanted to interest him in; here was her opportunity, Miss Frayle thought, as she came quickly forward. There could be no more appropriate moment to interrupt him and tell him about what she had experienced at the dentist's.

'Oh, Dr. Morelle — ' she said again; but he still did not, or refused to hear her.

'But then,' Dr. Morelle was asking, 'you know what Theodor Reik has to say on the matter of dreams?'

Professor Kane murmured something to the effect that unfortunately he was not acquainted with Mr. Reik's profound utterances on the subject, and that Miss Frayle appeared anxious to interrupt the proceedings; but Dr. Morelle had not waited to hear his query answered.

'He quotes the case of the dancer,' Dr. Morelle said smoothly, 'who in a dream performed a dance which was greeted by the audience's enthusiastic applause, except for someone shouting out that the dancer was not keeping time to the music. You would imagine this situation would offer a perfectly obvious interpretation: something concerned with her profession. But, of course, the analyst has learned to mistrust the obvious and appropriate, the superficial and logical in the matter of dream-interpretation — '

Miss Frayle gave another cough; if she failed to get a word in edgeways now, she was convinced she might never again be presented with such a suitable opportunity to speak to him about Tod Hafferty. 'Oh — er — Dr. Morelle — ' she said.

Professor Kane did his best to help her attract Dr. Morelle's attention. 'Dr. Morelle,' he said, 'I think Miss Frayle wants a word with you — '

'Which is precisely where the criminologist can profit by comparing his methods of investigation with that of the psychoanalyst,' Dr. Morelle sailed on.

Miss Frayle sighed and gave up; Professor Kane gave a little shrug of sympathy in her direction. 'When the detective encounters evidence,' Dr. Morelle was continuing, 'which offers an obvious explanation, then is the occasion for him to recall the case Theodor Reik recalls, that of the dancer and her dream.'

He paused, but Miss Frayle made no attempt to speak; she was past it now. Let him rattle on, she thought a trifle bitterly, she would have to try and jump in some other time; or forget the whole thing. It probably wasn't all that important, anyway.

'Because, of course,' Dr. Morelle said, 'the dancer's dream had no relation to her professional work whatsoever; it arose directly out of the fact that at the time of her marriage, she had been a virgin.'

'Oh,' Professor Kane said, and then with a glance at Miss Frayle, he managed to put in: 'Er — Dr. Morelle, Miss Frayle — '

But his words were as wasted as they had been before; Dr. Morelle went on: 'Her dream of the dance that a member of the audience cried out that she was out of step was merely the surface, artificial and deceptive, the same as one might encounter in the case of a pond whose abysmal depths are hidden by an enticingly green mask of weed.' He paused, smugly pleased with the parallel he had drawn. 'So the surface of this dream concealed the truth the dancer's inner conflict of sexual emotions and inhibitions — '

There came a sudden movement behind Miss Frayle, and she turned to see Professor Kane's housekeeper, her face shiny with anxiety; and behind her she recognized the familiar form of P.C. Jarrett, as he pushed his way past the housekeeper and said:

'Dr. Morelle, I wonder if you could help, please?'

At once Dr. Morelle swung on his heel, his somewhat startling elucidation of the dancer's dream to be indefinitely postponed as he eyed the uniformed figure with a raised eye-brow.

'It's Major Kelly,' Jarrett said. 'He — he's gone and cut his throat.'

14

Dr. Morelle and the sharp-featured man who was Detective-Inspector Arnold of Sandwich C.I.D., together with P.C. Jarrett, sat round a table in the front-room which was the office at Eastmarsh police-station. It was 1.25 p.m., and P.C. Oxley had brought in sandwiches from the nearby public-house, and made plenty of hot coffee, before going off on his own routine duties.

When Fay Kelly with an expression on her face he had never seen before on any young woman's face, came rushing out to the chalk-pit to tell him incoherently of her father's death, P.C. Jarrett had taken her straight to Inspector Arnold. While the latter listened to her, Jarrett mentioned that Dr. Morelle was staying nearby and what about calling him in? The police-surgeon from Sandwich having completed his part of the job for the present respecting Tod Hafferty had returned to police-headquarters.

'Okay,' Inspector Arnold had said to Jarrett, who had promptly hurried to Professor Kane's bungalow. Inspector Arnold went with Fay Kelly back to Roselands.

His restful weekend disintegrating all around him, Dr. Morelle had gone at once with Jarrett to the Kelly's house, where the daily help was doing her best to comfort an hysterical Nola Kelly. Dr. Morelle and Jarrett went straight to the bathroom where Inspector Arnold was waiting.

'Classical case of suicide,' Dr. Morelle had said to Inspector Arnold, while Jarrett had done his best not to keep his gaze averted from the figure collapsed over the bath. 'You will observe,' Dr. Morelle had continued, 'that the throat-wound is in such a position that it could be easily effected, indicative that the person was not mentally deranged at the time of death. Note that the wound begins under the left ear and extends obliquely across the throat to the right. This man was obviously right-handed.'

Dr. Morelle glanced at the C.I.D. detective, who nodded his head in agreement.

'If the wound had run in the opposite direction,' Dr. Morelle went on, 'a strong suspicion of murder might be entertained. Especially if there was blood on the back of the neck and the shoulders; or again, if the wound extended to the vertebrae. You will observe, too, that this man had undone his necktie and collar preparatory to committing the deed, an almost invariable action in suicide-cases. If this had not been apparent, and the shirt-collar had been cut through, again suspicion of murder might arise.'

Dr. Morelle blew out a spiral of cigarette-smoke. 'I recall a case where the murderer had untied his victim's collar to give the impression it was suicide, after he had stabbed him; but, of course, the collar was already cut by the knife, so that his ruse was obvious.'

There was no doubt that it was suicide, committed with the old-fashioned razor which Major Kelly habitually used, and which lay in the bath where it had fallen, in a river of blood.

Nola Kelly was utterly unable to answer any questions and Dr. Morelle sent her to bed, while the local doctor was phoned. Fay Kelly gave her story of how she had found her father.

It was Dr. Morelle who took her aside in the sitting-room and gradually drew from her all she knew about Nola Kelly's liason with Tod Hafferty.

'This knowledge, to which was added the shock of learning of Tod Hafferty's death, could have caused him to take his own life?' he asked her.

'What else could it have been?'

Dr. Morelle had no alternative to offer her. He had left her to await the arrival of the doctor, and to look after her mother.

Then, with Inspector Arnold, he had gone to the chalk-pit and viewed that other body, before it was removed in the same ambulance which took Major Kelly away. All the photographs had been taken, while the search continued; nothing had been found in the vicinity of the chalk-pit which had any bearing on the one-time film-star's death.

No trace of the heavy stick or club which had obviously been used to batter him over the head; he had been struck several times from behind. But whatever it was that had been used, the assailant would have had no difficulty in disposing of it, either by burying it quickly under the rubbish in the chalk-pit, or hiding it in the nearby undergrowth. It would be a mere matter of luck if the stick or club came to light.

Now, in the police-station office, over their sandwiches and coffee they were debating the obvious question: did Major Kelly's suicide supply the answer to Tod Hafferty's murder?

From what Fay Kelly had told Dr. Morelle, her father had a motive for murdering his wife's lover that stuck out like a sore thumb; and the theory that he had been unable to face the shock of the discovery of Tod Hafferty's body fitted perfectly with his then taking his own life.

'It fits okay,' Inspector Arnold said for the second time; and Jarrett nodded his agreement.

He himself was only just beginning to

regain some of his composure, shattered both by Fay's rush out of the house and the sight that had met his eyes in the bathroom. A man missing, followed by murder and a suicide all within twenty-four hours was outside the routine of a village policeman. He still didn't feel enthusiastic about lunch, and had watched with envious incredulity while Inspector Arnold ate his way through the sandwiches as if he might never eat again.

'That's the trouble,' Dr. Morelle said through a cloud of cigarette-smoke.

Inspector Arnold washed down the last mouthful of his sandwich with a gulp of coffee, and looked at Dr. Morelle.

'It fits,' Dr. Morelle said, 'except for the fact that more than one person would appear to have been concerned with Hafferty's death.'

Jarrett stared at him.

'How do you know there was someone else?' Inspector Arnold said.

Dr. Morelle glanced at P.C. Jarrett. 'At what time yesterday evening did you and Charles Hafferty view the chalk-pit?'

'Approximately 6.45 p.m.'

'And there was no sign of Tod Hafferty's body, then?'

'No,' Jarrett said slowly.

Dr. Morelle turned to the detective-inspector. 'Your estimate is that he was killed at approximately 6 p.m.?'

The other nodded. 'Our saw-bones worked it out that he'd been dead approximately thirteen hours; he was found at 7.15 a.m.' He referred to some notes beside his coffee-cup. '*Rigor mortis* was complete; and taking into account the low atmospheric temperature, I'd say his estimate makes sense.'

Dr. Morelle nodded. 'Precisely. Which would indicate that he was killed elsewhere first, and then conveyed to the chalk-pit.'

Inspector Arnold rubbed his chin with a large, neatly manicured hand. 'That's a possibility I hadn't taken into account,' he said. 'In which case, where was he done in, and why was he moved?'

'There's only one thing,' P.C. Jarrett said hesitantly. 'He may have been there all the time. In the chalk-pit, I mean.'

Dr. Morelle's eyes beneath his dark

brows glittered. His expression made it clear that he had so far mentioned only one possibility which could support his theory that more than one person had been involved in the murder.

'But you said you and Charles Hafferty gave the place the once-over at about 6.45 p.m.' Inspector Arnold looked at the other, who shifted uncomfortably.

'It was dark,' he said, 'we could have missed spotting the body with our torches; it was daylight when he was found. He couldn't have been missed then.'

'I see.'

'Alternatively,' Dr. Morelle said, 'Charles Hafferty may have deliberately avoided seeing it.'

The detective-inspector eyed him shrewdly. 'You mean none so blind as those who don't want to see.' He turned to Jarrett. 'Can you recall anything which was suspicious about Charles Hafferty?'

Jarrett tried to recall the search of Asshe Woods and the vicinity of the chalk-pit. He remembered the brambles scratching their clothes, and how they had walked, swinging their torches from side to side, each by mutual understanding taking his own area to cover. There had been the broken wire fence a yard or two from the edge of the graveyard of petrol-cans and holed buckets.

Was it possible, he wondered for the other man to have carefully distracted his attention from the spot where Tod Hafferty's body lay all the time?

'I suppose he could have done it,' he said to Inspector Arnold.

'Has he got an alibi for the relative time?' the C.I.D. man asked.

'I'll find out,' Jarrett said.

'Do just that.'

'At any rate,' Dr. Morelle said, 'we can be sure it wasn't a tramp or ordinary thief who committed the crime.'

'How is that, Dr. Morelle?' Jarrett said.

'What thief would have left the dead man's gold wrist-watch and note-case with money?'

Jarrett caught Inspector Arnold's slightly pitying expression and went a little red in the face. That should have been obvious to him. 'I see what you mean,' he muttered. 'Of course.' He wasn't appearing too bright.

'Whoever killed him,' Inspector Arnold was saying, 'knew he invariably took that walk at that particular time, and was waiting for him.' He massaged his chin again. 'That could fit in very well with his son, Charles. There remains the motive. Elder sons have taken a poor view of their parents before now.'

The room was warm, the air heavy with the aroma of Dr. Morelle's cigarette. Oustide, the brightness of the February afternoon had faded; it was grey and chill. There was a small front-garden, and a young tree scraped a leafless branch against the window.

'Post-mortem should pin-point the time of death pretty exactly, eh, Dr. Morelle?' Inspector Arnold said. 'According to how far the lunch in his stomach had digested.'

Jarrett suppressed a wince, and wondered if it was up to him to mention having seen Fay Kelly watching from the garden of Roselands. But he felt convinced it couldn't have any possible bearing on the murder, and remained silent. It was then that he became aware of Dr. Morelle quietly watching him; his eye seemed to be fixed on him mesmerically, as if impelling him to say something. To speak of the girl with Hafferty in the railway compartment?

He was reminded of it with a jolt that was almost physical. He blinked at Dr. Morelle, and swallowed uncomfortably. What sort of a police-officer was he turning out to be? First, he was saying nothing about Fay Kelly, because he tried to tell himself it was irrelevant; while all the time he knew he was really anxious not to involve her more than was absolutely necessary in this dreadful business; and now he was saying nothing about this other girl. Why? Because it originated in his reluctance to besmirch the old-time film-star's name? Because he had assured himself that the girl had no connection with what had happened to the old man?

Was he supposed to make this sort of judgment?

He knew well enough where his duty

lay; it was his job to reveal all he knew about everything that could have any possible relevance to the case under investigation.

'This had better be your department,' he heard Inspector Arnold saying. 'You know all the people around Asshe, none better. So you'd better hop on that bike of yours and check the alibi of everyone you think we ought to have. It should be just your cup of tea.'

P.C. Jarrett swallowed again, and muttered his acquiescence. He gave Dr. Morelle a quick glance. That mesmeric look still fixed him.

'Let's list those I want,' the detective-inspector said briskly. 'Charles Hafferty, for a kick-off; and his wife.' He had sent his detective-sergeant to Asshe House earlier that morning, for a brief chat with Charles Hafferty, to obtain a picture of the dead man's movements yesterday and his general habits. 'Then Nicky Hafferty,' he went on. 'The married daughter, what's her name — ?'

'Olivia Parker,' Jarrett said.

'And her husband,' Arnold said.

'Bill Parker,' Jarrett said. 'The estate-agent.'

'Who else? The widow, I suppose. You'll treat her gently; and there's Mrs. Kelly and the daughter. You might dig something out of them that could be useful. But you'll have to go easy there, too.'

'Mrs. Kelly will be unable to say anything,' Dr. Morelle said, 'for several days.'

He had seen her with the family doctor, kept quiet only by sedatives, sleeping fitfully in her darkened room. She had refused to have a nurse to look after her; Fay Kelly, despite the terrific shock she herself had suffered, remained on hand all the time, taking a nurse's place. It helped her, she had told Dr. Morelle, to keep her mind off that ghastly sight in the bathroom.

'You'd better keep away from there, then,' Inspector Arnold said, 'until you've checked with me first; I'll be in touch with her doctor.'

'Right,' Jarrett said. 'Then there's Alf Layton, and — '

'That's the handyman, isn't it? And

Bess — what's her other name?'

'Bess Pinner,' Jarrett said. 'She's been there since when.'

'Anyway, that seems to be about the lot,' Inspector Arnold said. 'Work your way through them as soon as you can; and if we think of anyone else . . . ' He shrugged. 'I leave it to you,' he added, 'to tackle them in whichever order you think.'

Jarrett nodded, and the other got to his feet. Jarrett stood up politely. The Sandwich C.I.D. man looked at Dr. Morelle who still sat, contemplating the tip of his Le Sphinx.

'Don't know that there's much left for us to discuss,' Inspector Arnold said. 'I'll get back to the chalk-pit, to see if anything has come up about the murder-weapon; and then I shall return to Sandwich; they ought to have the result of the autopsy. That may tell us something new.' He gave Dr. Morelle another look. 'Very grateful to you for your invaluable help.'

Dr. Morelle regarded him urbanely. 'Never can resist the lure of a crime-investigation, no matter where it takes place. In the heart of a metropolis or in a remote village, it holds a magnetic appeal to me.'

He still sat at the table, a half-full coffee-cup at his elbow, a half-eaten sandwich before him. Inspector Arnold eyed him curiously. 'You mean because the dead man's an ex-film-star or something? It gives it all a sort of glamour?'

Dr. Morelle took a drag at his cigarette and the other two watched the tip glow and pulsate like a living coal from the fire burning in the grate.

He said, as if he hadn't heard Inspector Arnold: 'There's something about this business, some odd flavour.'

'Quite,' Inspector Arnold said.

'No, not glamour,' Dr. Morelle continued, thoughtfully. 'I've seen enough of that to know it for its true value. No; more likely something to do with the dog.'

'Hero?' P.C. Jarrett said. His face lit up with pleasure at the idea of Dr. Morelle's interest in his dog.

Dr. Morelle contemplated him quizzically. 'I can't recall a case before in which

I have participated, where canine intelligence as well as my own was introduced in an effort to elucidate the mystery.'

'I'm afraid I wasn't able to use him to any effect,' Jarrett said. He began to explain the circumstances which last night had militated against the Alsatian's special qualities, when Inspector Arnold interrupted him.

'You know what your duties are for the rest of the day,' he said. 'I'll be getting along.' He gave Dr. Morelle a brisk, businesslike smile. 'Again, many thanks.'

Dr. Morelle and P.C. Jarrett watched him from the front-gate drive off in the police-car which had arrived for him by pre-arrangement. Jarrett followed Dr. Morelle back into the police-station. They faced each other in the office and Jarrett said: 'What's on your mind, Dr. Morelle? I mean, you don't want to listen to any more about my blessed dog?'

'I rather imagine,' Dr. Morelle said smoothly, 'that you may be more interested to hear what I have to say to you about the girl you saw with Tod Hafferty.'

15

So this, P.C. Jarrett thought, was what lay behind Dr. Morelle's apparent interest in Hero? It had merely been a device to cover up his interest in something else, while Inspector Arnold was there. Now the detective-inspector was gone, Dr. Morelle could talk more freely. What he had on his mind was something he did not want Inspector Arnold to hear. Something to do with Tod Hafferty and the girl?

Frank Jarrett took a deep breath.

It was all crowding in on him a bit too much. Yes, he was interested in people, all right; that was what he had thought: people, not the rural life around him. But he was beginning to realize that human beings were not so simple to deal with all the time. He was beginning to think that the flower-shows and village-fêtes had a lot to recommend them. Oh, yes, people aroused his interest and his feelings of warm goodwill towards them. But not when they got themselves mixed up with murder and suicide.

He looked at Dr. Morelle with mingled envy and admiration. He'd got it all taped; human beings and their unpredictability were nothing new to him, whatever size they came in, he had their measure. Jarrett wondered what it was that Dr. Morelle had learned about the girl and Tod Hafferty.

'As you surmised,' Dr. Morelle was saying, 'the object of my interest in your dog was a pretext. It occurred to me we should be able to talk more easily out of Inspector Arnold's hearing.'

'I still haven't said anything to him about Friday afternoon,' Jarrett said. 'Or about meeting the girl again last night.' He hesitated, then he said: 'I mean, when I told you about it, you didn't say you thought it was all that important.'

'As I recall it,' Dr. Morelle smiled at him frostily, 'I offered no comment one way or the other. It was a matter entirely for you.'

The other nodded. 'I suppose it looked

a bit suspicious, her being near Asshe House at that time. What could she be doing there, and the old boy dead?'

Dr. Morelle took a cigarette from his slim gold case; his lighter flared and he said through a haze of cigarette-smoke: 'This part of the world is a small world, where the long arm of coincidence has even less far to reach than in the metropolis.'

Jarrett recalled the aroma which he had sniffed on the moonlit air last night, the intriguing scent of Dr. Morelle's Egyptian cigarette. 'You think it had nothing to do with the murder?'

'Her presence in the vicinity would indicate her innocence of any knowledge of the crime, rather than the reverse?'

'You think so?' There was a note of wishful thinking in the other's tone.

'If she possessed any knowledge that Tod Hafferty was lying murdered in the nearby chalk-pit, is it likely that she would deliberately show herself in the vicinity? On the contrary, she would keep well away.' The other made no reply. His brows were drawn together in perplexity.

'As it happens,' Dr. Morelle said, 'you may rest assured that she had nothing to do with his death.'

Jarrett's head came up with a jerk. He had caught the note of certainty in Dr. Morelle's voice. 'How do you know?'

'She told me,' Dr. Morelle said laconically.

'You've seen her, yourself?'

Dr. Morelle nodded. 'I mentioned the long arm of coincidence,' he said. He tapped the ash off the end of his Le Sphinx and bestowed on the other an enigmatic smile. 'Do not despise it. Where would the detective be without some assistance from coincidence?'

'What — what did she say?'

Briefly Dr. Morelle described his visit to the derelict harbour at Richborough, and his meeting with the girl in the tumbledown hut on the deserted waste of silt and weed, rotting jetties and rusting steel. 'She had no hesitation in mentioning that she had been near Asshe House at the time you said you had seen her. She explained that Tod Hafferty had failed to keep a pre-arranged rendezvous with her in the woods that afternoon.'

P.C. Jarrett mumbled something; his mouth was slightly open. He had not recovered from his surprise over Dr. Morelle's disclosure that he had actually met the girl and gained her confidence.

'I thought it wiser that she should not know that you had reported having seen her,' Dr. Morelle added. 'Instead, I pretended I had noticed her myself last night.'

'Yes; and I won't mention that I've discussed her with you.'

Dr. Morelle's expression was urbane. 'When do you expect to be interrogating her yourself?' he asked softly.

Jarrett felt himself reddening. He had not intended to convey that he felt it necessary to check with the girl himself. 'I — I didn't mean,' he stammered, 'that there would really be any need to confirm what she told you. About her not being implicated in Hafferty's murder, I mean. What she told you must be the truth, of course. You'd know that.'

'I'm glad I have earned your confidence,' Dr. Morelle said.

P.C. Jarrett could feel the perspiration beading his hot brow, but he managed to restrain himself from mopping his face with a handkerchief.

'What I'm trying to say,' he blurted out, 'is: what should I do about her, now you've told me what you have?' Dr. Morelle offered no comment, and the other went on. 'You know I ought really have reported that business between the pair of them in the train, only I didn't because I just couldn't stomach the idea of the disgrace and mud-slinging the poor devil would endure.'

'A perfectly understandable conflict between what you understand to be your duty,' Dr. Morelle said, 'and compassion for a fellow-creature.'

Jarrett nodded and swallowed noisily. He felt a little cooler; he could feel the sweat drying off round his temples. 'But now,' he said earnestly, 'the old boy's been done in, and — and, well, she might know something about it. She might give us a lead — '

'But you can't satisfy yourself in this respect,' Dr. Morelle cut in incisively, 'without disclosing to Inspector Arnold that you had omitted to report evidence of their illicit liaison?'

P.C. Jarrett swallowed again, less noisily this time. 'That's the spot I'm in,' he said.

Dr. Morelle stubbed out his cigarette, and glanced out of the window, against which the branch-tip still scraped. Jarrett caught the purposeful line of his lean jaw silhouetted against the grey shadows of the afternoon. It was as if, the young policeman decided, Dr. Morelle had some secret line of action planned and was anxious to follow it without delay. The saturnine profile turned and the dark, boring gaze bent upon him.

'The solution to your dilemma seems clear,' Dr. Morelle said. 'It is simply this, that you inform Inspector Arnold that it was I who had advised you how I had observed her last night.'

'Why, yes,' Jarrett said, brightening. 'If I can say that.'

'No need for you to refer to what you know about her and Hafferty; you immediately recognized her from the

189

information I gave you, upon which you acted.'

'Thanks a lot, Dr. Morelle.'

Dr. Morelle shrugged. 'I would be gratified,' he said, 'if, you would continue to keep the matter of our co-operation secret from her.'

'Of course,' P.C. Jarrett said hurriedly.

'I should not like her to have the impression that I have acted the copper's nark.'

'I understand.'

Jarrett found himself wondering if this meant that Dr. Morelle himself intended to improve upon his acquaintance with the girl, and there came into his mind the image of her, youthful and vibrant, with brash, flashy sexuality. Did Dr. Morelle find her attractive, as the unfortunate Tod Hafferty had done? It was a momentary question which flashed across his consciousness, so that he barely had time to dismiss it as unworthy and un-called for.

'So far as I know, I have no intention of seeing her again,' Dr. Morelle was saying, as if in answer to his brief conjecture. 'But, as you suggested, she may still produce some lead which you might find of interest to pursue.'

He moved to the door. 'You're going, are you, Dr. Morelle?'

'There is not much I can do here, it's left in your capable hands, and those of Inspector Arnold. I intend driving up to London.'

'London?'

P.C. Jarrett frowned at him. What might there be up in London that could have any bearing on the case? He opened his mouth to ask, then decided against it. It suddenly occurred to him that Dr. Morelle might have learned more from the girl than he had thought necessary to reveal to anyone else. Jarrett now experienced the distinct impression that Dr. Morelle's manner had been some-what secretive when he had described the outcome of that meeting with her in the hut at the old harbour. Had he withheld certain information which he had acquired for some ulterior purpose?

Or was he merely imagining it, in retrospect? What purpose, he asked himself, could Dr. Morelle have that was different from that of the police? His object must be identical, the discovery of Tod Hafferty's murderer.

He glanced at Dr. Morelle, his look questioning but it remained unanswered. Dr. Morelle might not have seen it, or heard his query, as he turned to the door, and threw over his shoulder: 'I expect to be back late tonight; if you should want to get into touch with me, you will find Miss Frayle at Professor Kane's home.'

He was gone, and a few moments later there came the deep-throated roar of the Duesenberg as it headed in the direction of Asshe, and London.

P.C. Jarrett gave a long sigh, and then set about deciding how best to follow Inspector Arnold's instructions. He sat down at the table and began making a list in his note-book.

Charles Hafferty.

Marie Hafferty. Jarret's pencil hovered over the name as he wrote it down, his thoughts filling with that plump, seductive figure and its sensual invitation in every curve.

Nicky Hafferty.

His sister, Olivia, married to Bill Parker.

Bill Parker, the estate-agent. His office was at the other end of Eastmarsh; two rooms converted from the ground-floor of a private house. There was a flat overhead, occupied by an old married couple. Parker employed a young girl from a little village this side of Sandwich as secretary. A dumpy little thing with a reddened nose. As he noted Bill Parker's name, Jarrett idly recalled noticing lately a light in his office sometimes burning late, and at weekends.

Then there was Mrs. Hafferty; go easy with her, Inspector Arnold had said.

And go easy with the other widow, Mrs. Kelly.

That left Fay Kelly. Frank Jarrett shifted uneasily as he added her name to the list, as into his mind came the image of her watching from the moon-lit garden of Roselands. He had held back on that little incident, too, he reminded himself. He shook his head decisively; it was of no importance, he felt certain. She had explained it to him last night. It was simply, as she had said, idle curiosity arising out of sheer boredom attracted by the torch-lit shadows of the search-party.

But Fay Kelly's face still filled his mind as he went out, pulling on his overcoat, and pausing to say a word to Hero, got his bicycle.

16

Marie Hafferty stared out of the sitting-room window of Woodview, making up her mind that a hot bath and a book by the fire were the only possible ways to spend the evening. Unless Nicky was at home. If he was in a good humour they might play cards. She enjoyed gambling. For her there was colour and excitement hidden in a pack of playing-cards. When she played she could dream she was in a different setting, elegantly dressed with wealthy, shrewd-faced men across the table, and high stakes.

Charles wasn't interested; he preferred to pore over art-books, when he wasn't working in his studio at the back of the house.

She looked out across the garden, where the daylight was fading. Within half-an-hour night would have shrouded the scene. A terrible restlessness swept over her. There was an intolerable quality in these weekends at the end of the day. The light seemed to linger with a special, taunting brightness. She could not believe that spring was not far away, only that there was the bitterness of February and March still to be lived through.

Her thoughts jerking back to Nicky, she turned into the room and began switching on the electrically-fitted old-fashioned oil-lamps. She drew the curtains and then went into the kitchen, very modern and gleaming, and she put the kettle on and lit up a cigarette. The steady tick of the clock on the wall was the only sound in the house. She glanced at the clock and frowned. Charles was spending all his time at Asshe House. Almost as if his father's death had provided him with a wonderful excuse for remaining away from his own home.

She supposed it was natural enough for him to want to hang around the house while his mother lay in a state of collapse. She had taken it terrifically badly, and Charles was worried that she would never get over it. Even though the family doctor had reassured him that time would take care of it all. What a fool he would look, Marie thought idly, if his mother married again. Her thoughts turned to Nola Kelly. She wouldn't stay a widow long, that was a certain bet.

Irritably Marie made the tea. Nicky ought to be in soon. She knew she spent too much time thinking about Nicky. She was clear-eyed enough to realize she was only building up to a lot of unhappiness for herself, but she was bored enough too to take the risk of it. For a few moments of pleasure with Nicky she was prepared to gamble months of sulky, unspoken recriminations from Charles, she told herself; she would suffer a whole future of slights from Nicky himself. She put her hands up to her breasts and gave a low moan. Sometimes her body ached and cried out for physical pleasure.

The rat-tat at the front-door startled her. She was not easily scared, but people didn't often knock at her door. There weren't many strangers around in Asshe. She gulped some tea, went out into the hall, switching on the lights, and flung the door open.

P.C. Jarrett said: 'I was on my way back; I thought you might be in.'

She let out her breath in a long sigh. 'Come in,' she invited, and stood aside to let him pass. 'There's a cup of tea in the kitchen,' she said.

He followed her into the warmth and brightness, and he sighed and visibly relaxed; 'I won't keep you a minute or two,' he said. 'Just a few points I'd like to clear up.'

She shut the door and leaned her back against it, smiling faintly.

'I'm afraid my husband isn't back yet. He's over at Asshe House.'

He interrupted her as she started to explain Charles's anxiety for his mother. 'I've already seen him,' he said. 'I guessed he might be there.'

'I see,' she said. 'You'd better have a cup of tea. You look a bit tired.' He looked keyed-up she thought, his face tense, with a look in his eyes she couldn't fathom, a kind of bleak, frozen look.

'Thanks. I didn't bother your husband too much. As you said, he's worried about Mrs. Hafferty. And I think there's some delayed-action shock over his father's death.'

'So you thought you'd see what you could dig out of me?' She gave him a look that was meant to be melting and inviting. 'You think I'm tough, and can take sudden death without feeling anything.'

'Not at all, Mrs. Hafferty,' he said.

'You can call me Marie,' she said. 'What's your name?'

He told her, stammering a little, and she laughed throatily at his embarrassment. 'It's all right,' she said, 'I'm not going to seduce you. Even though you are attractive. For a cop, anyway.'

She pushed the cup of tea across the table and watched him drink. She could see a little composure return into his face. 'Here, sit down,' she said.

He slumped into the chair and sat gazing round the kitchen, feeling her eyes on him. 'I hope I'm not intruding,' he muttered, for want of something better to say.

'You been biking round all afternoon?' she said. 'Checking up on what people know about the murder?'

He nodded, and undid the buttons of his overcoat. He fixed his gaze on the new-type stove, the front of which was open and the fire gleamed redly through the bars. He heard her speaking about Major Kelly's suicide, and did he think it had anything to do with Tod Hafferty's death. He gave a non-committal answer over the rim of his tea-cup.

'When do you finish for the day?' she said.

'Don't suppose there'll be any knocking off for any of us till this business is cleared up.'

'Have you got anywhere at all?' she said.

'Not so far as I know,' he said. 'But I'm only a small cog in the investigation. Just collecting what information I can from anyone. Routine stuff.'

She said softly: 'All right, so I'm nosy. But you know anything you tell me won't go any further. I like to hear gossip, but I don't spread it.'

That was what women always said, he told himself. Then he looked at her more sharply. It occurred to him that there was an air of commonsense about her; she wasn't trying to ram her sexuality down his throat, not for the moment, anyway. He suddenly realized that it was agreeable sitting here in this comfortable kitchen, with its breakfast table in the corner, high-backed chairs and decorative dresser. Perhaps what she said was reasonably true. She did enjoy gossip, and collected it without yapping too much in return. She was the type, too, he ruminated, who would give some thought to people's characters and motives.

'Is there anyone in particular who's come under suspicion?' she was saying. Her face had suddenly come alive. She sat down facing him across the table. He put down his tea-cup, shaking his head.

'Not really,' he said. He thought he might as well appear enigmatic. It might intrigue her and help persuade her to tell him what she knew. If she knew anything at all. 'Do you know anyone who might have wanted Mr. Hafferty out of the way?'

'That would be telling.'

Her eyes dropped slyly, and he grinned at her. Two could play at pretending to be enigmatic, he realized. Was that all she was interested in, so far as he was concerned, just flirting with him? Or more, if he played up to her?

'After all, I am a police-officer,' he said, mock-seriously. 'If there's anything you know that you think I ought to know, it's your duty to tell me.'

'I think you ought to know that you're rather attractive,' she said, and laughed out loud as he went red in the face. Then her expression hardened and she leaned across the table. He managed not to draw back at the nearness of her, the unashamedly thrusting curve of her breasts. 'How can you stick this God-forsaken hole?' she grated through white teeth. 'Is this your idea of Life with a capital L? You want to know something — Frank?' Her tone softened over his name. 'Oh, it's nothing to do with Tod Hafferty's death — he got what was coming to him, anyway. But do you know sometimes I wish I could get on a train, set my feet on a London street, and never see the trees and fields ever again.'

'What would you do with yourself?'

'I'd find myself a man with a lot of money, and I'd have a damn good time,' she said loudly. 'One helluva whale of a time.'

It seemed a pretty pathetic sort of ambition, he reflected, to feel so strongly about. All he said was: 'Well, perhaps you'll get your wish.'

'What do you mean by that?' she said sharply.

He saw the sudden fury jump into her eyes and he wondered what he could have said that had irritated her. He decided that she didn't like being taken too seriously. 'Nothing really,' he said vaguely. 'Only if your father-in-law's money is shared out among the family, you ought to get a bit.' She sat very still. 'Sorry if I upset you. Let's change the subject, anyway.'

Her mood changed abruptly and she smiled at him. 'It's all right,' she said. 'I'm sick of people who don't say what's in their minds. At least you're honest.' She gave him a long intent look. 'I suppose you have to be if you're a cop.'

'It's supposed to help,' he said. He eyed the tea remaining in his cup. He cleared his throat before he said slowly: 'What makes you think he only got what was coming to him?'

He made it sound as casual as he could, while he kept a faintly amused, disbelieving smile fixed on his face. Maybe she could be useful to him, but once she suspected he put any reliance on what she had to tell him, he'd never see the back of her, she'd always be chasing after him. He decided that her reply would provide a test, whether she knew anything, or was just kidding him along for her personal, very personal, ends. He realized grimly that anything she told him might be no more than an effort to hook his interest with this ulterior motive at the back of it all.

'Did I actually say that?' she said. 'Well, I suppose I did. I agree I think it, I'm sure of it. Quite a few had it in for him.'

'Who, for instance?'

'The women, the young girls he seduced.'

There flashed across his mind with a cynical thought the picture of the old chap and the girl as he had witnessed them together. Difficult to say which was the seducer and which the seduced. He kept his ideas to himself, however. He heard her saying:

'You know about that, of course.' He shook his head. Her expression became disbelievingly amused. 'But everyone knew.'

'Perhaps you could name someone?' he said.

'What about Alf Layton's wife, for a start?'

He stared at her in astonishment. He had been expecting her to refer to Nola Kelly, she might easily have known something about that, since it was not a close secret locked in the hearts of the two lovers; or she might have learned about her father-in-law and the girl. He tried to recall what the wife of Alf Layton, the Hafferty's handyman, looked like. Then he remembered something about her not being a local woman, Alf Layton had met her when he had been in the army, during the war. A London girl, she'd been. He was picturing Alf Layton, short and thick-set, a local character type, with a fondness for a pint, but the sort of chap whose wife was attractive enough to ensnare Tod Hafferty? On the other hand, the old boy was fairly easy, his tastes ranged from a young slut under age of consent, to the svelte, sophisticated and lovely Nola Kelly. The wife of his own employee might have suited his book at one time.

'Did Alf Layton know?' he asked, while he continued furiously to recall if he'd ever seen Mrs. Layton.

Marie Hafferty shrugged her plump shoulders. 'He may not be such a local yokel as he looks,' she said.

'How do *you* know?'

Her dark eyes became veiled, then she leaned closer still to him, and caressed his arm with a smooth, well-shaped hand. 'I didn't say I knew,' she said. 'I only said what about his wife?' She paused and let her pointed tongue run round her full lower lip, leaving it moist, with a gleam of teeth, as she said: 'You will have to become more friendly if you want me to tell you what I know.'

'Now you're being coy.'

He drew back his arm from her fingers digging into the thickness of the navy-blue sleeve. 'Besides,' he reminded her, 'you said you didn't spread gossip. Either you know Alf Layton's wife and Tod Hafferty had an affair, or you only heard that they did.'

She hesitated, her face darkening. 'I saw him once,' she said slowly, as if the recollection was not particularly pleasant, 'leaving her house. It was one afternoon, the time when Alf Layton would be working. I saw Tod Hafferty look up at the bedroom-window, and she showed herself for a moment to wave at him.'

'He doesn't sound as if he was the discreet type exactly,' Jarrett said.

'He wasn't, very.'

He was remembering the way the old boy had acted with the girl; anyone seeing them together as they got on the train must have guessed they were up to no good. He heard Marie Hafferty saying: 'That's what makes me wonder — '

She broke off, and he waited for her to continue, frowning at her. 'What?'

'If someone was blackmailing him.'

'If they were, they would hardly have murdered him, would they?'

'I realize that,' she snapped. 'But I shouldn't be surprised if blackmail has got something to do with all this.' She stood up and he got to his feet. It was time for him to be getting along, anyway. 'Anyway,' she said, her gaze ranging boldly over him, 'if Alf Layton found out about his wife, he wouldn't be so friendly towards his boss, for a start.'

There was a movement at the door, which was half-open on to the hall, and Nicky Hafferty came into the kitchen. He stopped in his tracks at the sight of Jarrett, and his gaze whipped from him to his sister-in-law.

Jarrett thought he caught a fleeting panic rise in his eyes, then the newcomer said with assumed non-chalance: 'Oh, it's you.'

'Frank Jarrett was passing, and thought he'd just look in,' Marie Hafferty said.

'Are you kidding?'

Jarrett's jaw tightened into a hard line. He realized with a shock that he hated the blond good-looking youth who stood there negligently, his expression mocking his own less flamboyant, less moodily handsome appearance. It seemed that the other was openly comparing his enormous animal strength with Jarrett's slim, if wiry physique; Nicky Hafferty exulted in the fact that his bursting masculinity ran unchannelled, that no disciplinary bonds held him in.

P.C. Jarrett said, with a casualness he did not feel: 'Matter of fact, there are one or two points I'd like to check over with you, when you have the time.'

'I've got that, if I've got nothing else,' Nicky retorted. 'What do you want to know?' He stood with his arms crossed on his chest. Jarrett caught the look of disquiet that flickered across the woman's face.

'It's only about yesterday afternoon,' he said. 'I mean, perhaps you would fill it in for me. Where were you between, say, lunch and tea-time?'

'Out. But it's no business of yours where I went.'

'It's no good taking that attitude,' Marie Hafferty said quickly. But the other did not even glance at her.

'It's only a routine question,' Frank Jarrett said quietly, keeping his tone controlled, even though he could feel his pulse begin to race. 'It's nothing really important.'

'If it's so unimportant, then what did you ask me for? Anyway, I went for a walk.' Nicky was sneering sulkily. 'And I didn't see anyone. And no one saw me. Then I got on the bus and went to Sandwich and went to a couple of cafés, and a pub or two.'

'You mean, you were in a bit of a restless mood?' P.C. Jarrett said affably. Nicky Hafferty's glance was baleful, but the policeman seemed blissfully unconscious of it. 'So you were alone all afternoon and there's nobody who can vouch for your movements?' Jarrett stared at Nicky's blond profile, as the other swung himself away and lounged against the other corner of the table.

'Nobody at all, unless you want to dig out the bus clippie and ask her if she remembers me.'

He described her in lewd, searing phrases, while Marie Hafferty protested without avail. Then he swung round and peered into Jarrett's face, his blue eyes hard with fury. 'If you think I had anything to do with Tod's death, you're out of your tiny, stupid mind,' he said, and went out of the kitchen, slamming the door behind him with a crash that shook the house.

P.C. Jarrett felt like someone who throws a stone over a mountain-edge and starts off a landslide.

17

P.C. Jarrett was walking, pushing his bicycle, when he saw the girl in the pool of light from the lamp that projected from the high barn wall at the corner of the lane that ran down to a cluster of cottages, one of which was Alf Layton's. Jarrett's thoughts had been full of his encounter some fifteen minutes' back with Nicky Hafferty at Woodview, so that the sight of the figure approaching him failed to register for a moment.

She was walking briskly, her hands thrust deep into the pockets of her short overcoat. She moved into the beam of his bicycle-lamp, and he saw her spike-heeled shoes and sheer nylon stockings, the too-tight skirt. A gaudy head-scarf hid her hair. Her make-up was cleverly applied but she had probably put it on under artificial light, he thought, because her rouge and eye-shadow were far too thick.

She flashed him a ready-made, sexy

smile. 'Good evening, P.C. Jarrett,' she said. 'We do seem to be bumping into each other of an evening, don't we?'

'Good evening,' was all he said.

He would have passed her, even though in his confused state of mind, and remembering what Dr. Morelle had informed him about her, he felt that he ought to think of some excuse to stop and talk to her, when she stopped and said: 'I suppose I am right for the Parker's house, aren't I?'

Bill Parker and his wife occupied a smart-looking villa-type house halfway down a lane which he had just passed. It lay parallel with the lane he was approaching, where he would find Alf Layton's cottage. The two lanes formed two sides of the fields and paddocks to which the farmhouse beyond the barn-wall belonged.

'Straight on,' Jarrett said, automatically. 'On your left at the corner.'

'Oh, thanks ever so.' She switched the smile on again. She ran her eyes up and down him boldly and stood waiting.

'Are you a friend of theirs?' he heard

himself say. 'I mean, I don't expect Mrs. Parker is feeling up to visitors just at the moment.' He knew he sounded ridiculously pompous, and he could not think what had made him say what he had said to her. It was just the feeling that she made an impossible intrusion to the situation.

'Isn't she now?' She looked at him teasingly. 'I'm sure that's too bad.'

He thought he ought to make some effort to explain the reason for his spontaneous remarks. 'I mean — that is,' he said, 'she is suffering from a family bereavement.'

'Really? I don't see what it has to do with me,' the girl said, the smile gone from her face. Her eyes were hard, now, and unfriendly in the light from his bicycle-lamp.

He felt ineffectual and stupid; he had said something to the girl which was quite unnecessary, and which it was not up to him to say. Then he realized that he was trying to cover up his curiosity concerning her visit to Bill and Olivia Parker. Was this another link with Tod Hafferty's death? Yet the girl had asked him quite frankly for his help in directing her to the Parkers' house. Or was that a deliberately brazen attempt at covering up? She had seen him, she knew he had seen her. She may have decided her best bet was to bluff it out.

She gave a brittle laugh, which turned into a cough. 'I didn't know any policemen rode around on bikes these days,' she said, when the coughing fit was over. 'Most of them seem to have motor-bikes. Fancy having to pedal and push along these lonely roads.'

She had jabbed a needle into a tender spot. 'It's nice to know you're so interested in a village-cop's welfare,' he snapped at her. He got on his bicycle and rode off, his hands sweating, face red with suppressed anger. A few minutes later he was leaning his machine against the gate to Alf Layton's cottage. He went up the narrow path and knocked at the door. There was a light burning behind the cottage windows, and he saw a shadow pass over the drawn curtains, and then the door opened.

He found himself staring into the pretty face of a young woman, and he realized at once that this was Alf Layton's wife, and that he had seen her in Eastmarsh. He had felt quite surprised when he had learned who she was; it was then that he was told that she was a girl Alf Layton had met when he had been away soldiering.

'Oh,' she said to him breathlessly. She stood there holding the door open with one hand, while the other flew to her throat.

'Good evening, Mrs. Layton,' he said, adopting his best soothing tone.

She made no move to open the door and invite him in. He took off his helmet, and let a smile spread across his face. 'I — er — I just wondered if your husband was in.'

She shook her head. Still no movement of her arm that barred his way. It was a sun-tanned, rounded arm, he noted, where the sleeve was rolled up. She was wearing a smart little apron and a wisp of hair blew across her forehead.

'It's nothing important,' he said. 'I'm

just clearing up one or two things about yesterday afternoon. When poor Mr. Hafferty died. You know, where people were, and all that. I haven't been able to ask Alf yet; so perhaps you could tell me what you were both doing yesterday? Say, between lunch-time and tea.'

To his surprise, she suddenly looked thoroughly frightened. 'I don't really remember,' she said quickly. 'I think you ought to see Alf. He's sure to know.'

He spread his smile even wider. He made his tone warm with casual calm. 'I only wondered if you went out yesterday afternoon or anything like that.' Hell, he thought, you'd think she was suspected of doing-in Tod Hafferty.

'You'll have to see Alf, then,' she said. She was sullen, with eyes down-dropped. 'He'll be home at five.'

It was nearly five o'clock now, he thought. But she did not ask him in, to await her husband's return. He was frowning to himself, disbelief struggling with his recollection of what Marie Hafferty had told him about Alf Layton, and his wife. Looking at her now, petite and pretty against the warmth and brightness of the sitting-room, he needed little imagination to picture Tod Hafferty's reaction to the sight of her.

'You're not being very helpful, Mrs. Layton,' he said, trying not to sound impatient. Marie Hafferty may have put him on to something, after all. 'It's not as though anybody imagines either of you had anything to do with the tragedy.' He knew that she must have heard all about it from Alf Layton. 'Come on now, did you go out on Sunday afternoon or not? That's all I want to know.'

To his dismay she burst into noisy tears. She put her hands to her face, and swayed there, sobbing incoherently. For a moment, Jarrett had the idea of pushing past her into the sitting-room and then, slamming the door on them both, shaking the truth out of her. He was convinced now that Marie Hafferty had put him on to the track of Tod Hafferty's murderer.

Alf Layton.

Marie Hafferty had seen Tod Hafferty leaving this cottage, obviously after spending an illicit hour with this pretty woman who stood there now, weeping her heart out. Obviously Alf Layton had also found out, and taken his revenge. And Mrs. Layton knew all about it.

P.C. Jarrett managed to rein back on the impulse. After all, he reminded himself, it was Alf Layton out of whom he must drag the truth. He moved closer to the petite figure.

'Nothing to upset yourself over, Mrs. Layton,' he said. 'I'm sorry I've bothered you. I'll come back later when your husband's in and have a chat with him. Perhaps you'd like to let him know?' She muttered something into her handkerchief, and he replaced his helmet. 'You don't want him to find you crying over nothing at all, I'm sure.'

A few moments later he was striding towards the gate, every nerve quivering with excitement. He'd hit upon the identity of Tod Hafferty's killer, he knew it. All he had to do was to wait for him to put in an appearance. He reached his bicycle, closing the gate behind him, when a voice spoke to him out of the gloom.

'Now then, P.C. Jarrett — what have you been telling my wife about me?'

P.C. Jarrett twisted round and met the smiling face of Alf Layton.

'Oh, hello . . . '

Jarrett managed to control his voice, to sound as casually friendly as possible. He saw the other glance towards the door, at the same time as there came the click of the latch as Mrs. Layton shut it. Jarrett wondered if she had seen her husband's arrival. He would have thought she would have hurried out to try and warn him; it was the sort of panic action she might have been expected to take.

'I — I was just asking Mrs. Layton about one or two little things,' he said.

'Oh, yes?'

Alf Layton sounded perfectly at ease, just as he had been the previous night, when he had been with Jarrett and the other two searching the darkness around Asshe Woods. Jarrett wondered if he had cunningly managed to steer them away from the exact spot where the body had been found, later. He tried to recall anything suspicious about his movements then, but nothing came to mind that he could pin-point. He twisted his bicycle round so that the lamp illuminated Alf Layton's face.

'It was you I was asking about, really,' he said, his tone still quiet and controlled.

'Oh, yes?'

The short, stocky figure blinked up at him innocently.

'Yesterday afternoon,' Jarrett said. 'I'm just checking up to make sure where people were — yesterday afternoon.'

'You mean about the time that poor old devil was done in?'

Jarrett's eyebrows shot up. He rubbed his chin. 'Er — yes,' he said. 'Just routine checking, that's all. Your wife didn't seem quite sure where you'd got to. Or rather, she seemed to think I should ask you yourself.'

A look of profound embarrassment settled upon the other's face. He dropped his eyes and kicked at a loose stone by his feet. 'I didn't go out at all,' he said at last. 'No more did my wife. So you needn't bother with us, need you?'

'I ought to have some idea what you were doing.'

'Well, it's private,' Alf Layton said sullenly. The amiability had left his expression. 'I don't see how it's any concern of yours. I've told you we were indoors all afternoon, and that's enough.'

'I'm afraid it isn't, you know,' Jarrett said.

He thought he made it sound sufficiently grim; at any rate, it certainly had its effect. Alf Layton's sullenness dropped away. His eyes took on a gleam. 'Well,' he muttered, 'if I got to tell you, I got to tell you.'

'Afraid so.'

'Well, I was in bed — with Mrs. Layton.'

'All afternoon?'

P.C. Jarrett could feel the beads of perspiration sticking to the inside of his helmet, as he managed to frame the question.

'Why not?' Alf Layton growled at him. 'You seen my wife, ain't you? Wouldn't you like to spend all afternoon in bed with her? If you got the chance.'

Twenty minutes later, P.C. Frank Jarrett had propped his bicycle against the wall of Roselands and was making his way up the path to the front-door. He had called there earlier that afternoon, before his interview with Marie Hafferty. A nurse had answered his ring, and said that Fay Kelly had gone over to Sandwich, to obtain some special medicines from the chemist, it seemed, and would not be back for a couple of hours.

She had told him she thought that Fay Kelly had stood up to the shock of her father's death with extraordinary courage, and that, for the moment, anyway, she was behaving normally. But the reaction would set in during the next two or three days. He had left a message that he would call back later.

Fay Kelly herself opened the door to him this time. She looked pale, but managed to force the shadow of a smile into her eyes, as she asked him into the sitting-room. He followed her into the softly-lit, elegantly-furnished room, with its large gilt mirror over the bright fire. He could sniff the faint scent that he had

223

noticed before, Nola Kelly's. The scent of death that had caught his nostrils only that morning no longer hung on the air, though into his mind's eye came the picture of that stretcher-borne shape which had once been her father being carried into the ambulance, *en route* to Sandwich mortuary.

The girl's expression was composed, while he muttered some suitable words of sympathy, and inquiry after her mother. He tried not to sound too conventional, but she cut into his words with a sudden impatience. 'What do you want?' she said.

Her voice was low, and it struck him that the nurse had been right about her. She was still numbed with the shock of her encounter with sudden, violent death that morning. Its impact hadn't really got home. It was up to him, doing the job he was, to take fullest advantage of her frame of mind, and, if he could, trip her up into any admission that might prove useful to the investigation of the death of Tod Hafferty. If she was, in fact, in possession of more knowledge than she had so far offered.

His face became stiff as a board, his voice even more formal. 'Just making a few routine inquiries here and there.' He stood awkwardly, aware that she was looking him over. He hated the dark-blue overcoat he saw reflected in the mirror, the awkward-looking helmet he carried. This wasn't how he wanted her to see him. Oxley's wife had once said his uniform made him look handsome, but he knew it made him look pompous as well, and he didn't want to look pompous to Fay Kelly.

She took a cigarette from an ornate cigarette-box of heavy silver, and he fumbled to get out his lighter. Then he remembered he hadn't brought it; he hardly ever did carry it when he was in uniform. She had found some book-matches in her handbag and she bent her head to the flame and then drew smoke deeply into her mouth. It was very quiet, only the sound of footsteps overhead. The nurse, he supposed, going about her duties. Silence had fallen between them. Then she said:

'I didn't offer you a cigarette, because I

presume you are here on duty?'

He smiled at her. It was a smile which asked her not to rub it in, and her expression softened a little.

'It's a routine-call,' he said, 'and I'm sorry to have to bore you with it. After all you've gone through it's wonderful of you to let me come and see you.' He paused, but she had nothing to say. 'It's just this business of knowing where everyone was, yesterday afternoon.'

She stared at him. 'What do you want to know?'

'Just an idea where you were, that's all.' He tried to make his voice light. 'And your mother.'

'Mother?' She frowned. Then she gave a shrug. 'Suppose I refuse to tell you?'

'I'm sure you won't do that,' he said. He made himself smile, treat it as a joke, but he knew she wasn't joking.

'As for Mother,' she said, 'I haven't a clue where she was. I was out all yesterday afternoon, and I'll tell you I went out, but I won't tell you where, nor with whom, nor when I came back.'

He said unhappily: 'Please don't make

226

things difficult for yourself. You know I have to ask. You know it's not, well, personal curiosity. If what you say isn't relevant we'll forget all about it.' He heard the pomposity ring out in his voice and hated it. 'If you like,' he said, 'I'll leave it alone now. I'll come back some other time. Tomorrow, perhaps?'

She shook her head as if it couldn't matter less when he talked to her, now or some other time.

'I mean,' he went on, in another effort to appear helpful and sympathetic. 'It doesn't matter, really. It's only if you might have known of anyone or anything who might have had anything to do with Tod Hafferty and his death.'

'Don't be so stupid,' she flared out at him. 'If I had any idea that might help you about that I'd have told you.'

A weight rolled off his shoulders, he smiled, and suddenly she smiled back at him. For a second, then her face lost its light and she spoke in a flat voice.

'I had a date. In Asshe Woods. At three o'clock. Then I came home.'

A sickening jealousy gripped him. It

was like a body blow, but he had to go on as if he hadn't noticed. But his heart was pounding. 'I'm afraid it won't do,' he said.

Her face was suddenly grey and she began trembling violently, so that he was afraid she would collapse at his feet. He made a move towards her, but she drew back and held herself upright in an attitude of defiance. 'You asked me to tell you, and I will. You want to know where I was yesterday afternoon at the time when Tod Hafferty was murdered — '

'How did you know that was the relative time?' he said.

'What sort of moron do you take me for? You wouldn't be interested in knowing where people were then, unless that was the time he was murdered.'

He started to say something, but she went on inexorably, and he knew at that instant that whatever vague hopes he may have had about the possibility that she might feel any romantic interest in him, they had vanished there and then like a gambler's lucky streak.

'Where was I yesterday afternoon? I

was in Asshe Woods with Nicky Hafferty. That's not all. He asked me to marry him. I said no. Then he made love to me.' She added with bitter honesty: 'It wasn't rape, I could have stopped him, but I didn't.' He gave a gulp and she shot at him: 'And if that isn't a good enough alibi for both of us, perhaps you can dream up a better one.'

18

It was still dark when Frank Jarrett woke. He lay for a moment looking up at the darkness, then rolled out of bed. The air in the room was chilly and he groped for the dressing-gown he had left on the foot of the bed, on the brass and iron rail.

He slipped into it and pushed his feet into slippers; he went across to the window and pulled the curtains back. There was a thin sliver of moon that came riding out of the clouds as he watched, bathing the silent houses in a cold, pale light. His bedroom was in front of the house and he could see frost sparkling on the tree below.

He was unrefreshed, still tired. A dull ache throbbed behind his eyes. The few hours of sleep had set the events of the previous day at a great distance. None of it seemed real. They were only an ugly dream. He thought of all those who were involved, however indirectly, in the business of Tod Hafferty's death. They would all be sleeping now, lying curled up for warmth in their winter beds, sighing, dreaming.

Except for one, the killer? Was he lying awake, sweating on the top line, wondering whether he would get away with it? What chance had they got of finding him? Half of the people who knew the dead man could have had a reason for wanting Tod Hafferty out of the way. All of them had the opportunity. The winter itself had conspired to help them, the grey daylight fading before a proper search could be made, the heavy dew foiling Hero; the locale itself, rough and wild, hiding any footprint or trail to help the police.

Jarrett shivered. A bitter chill seemed to bite at his flesh. He looked longingly across at the bed, but he knew he could not sleep, and there was nothing worse than lying awake.

He went quietly out of the bedroom and downstairs, tiptoeing, anxious not to wake Oxley. The kitchen was warm, the fire in the stove was still going and he stood near it.

He ought to feel keyed up, filled with a burning ambition to prove himself something better than a village policeman with routine responsibilities. At the start it had been an exciting challenge he had never hoped to encounter. But now it had gone sour on him. Now he wanted the whole thing over and done with and the peace of a dull, plodding existence.

Either I'm just a village copper, no more and no less, he thought, or I ought to try another job. It would never be the same again. Before, he had started each day with a certain amount of anticipation, the feeling of something impending. Something he knew might never arrive, but the very thought of it kicked off each day for him. Now it had happened.

He filled a kettle from the kitchen-tap and put it on the gas-stove. While he waited for it to boil he turned the grill on and toasted two slices of bread. The butter was so hard it would not spread and he manipulated it impatiently with the knife. Then he made the tea and poured himself a large cup of it. He pulled a chair close to the fire and stuck his feet out to the warmth as he ate and drank.

He caught sight of his reflection in the mirror over the mantelpiece. His face was youthfully determined, dedicated-looking almost. I am the police, he thought wryly. That's it, that's what they all think. I am the law, the upright one, the one who never shows fear, who has an answer for everything. My voice has to be sharpened to a tone of authority. My face has to be fixed in lines of sober dignity, my eyes must gleam with patient reproach. And then I go off duty and they permit me to relax. But they don't tell me how to turn myself into a man, cast off the priggish morality of my job. And even in my off-duty hours I have to be careful not to do anything that would sully my precious reputation.

His mind coiled itself round the image of Fay Kelly. He found no difficulty at all in picturing her with Nicky Hafferty held together in a convulsive embrace in Asshe Woods. The tea tasted bitter in his mouth, as bitter as his dreams had turned of what might have been for him and Fay Kelly. If he hadn't been a dreary village cop, he told himself, he might have been the one in the woods with her.

On his return to the police-station after that shattering scene with Fay Kelly, he had collected his thoughts sufficiently to phone through to Inspector Arnold at Sandwich.

He had passed on the results of his inquiries into the alibis of Charles Hafferty and his wife, Marie: the former explaining how he and she had come over to Asshe House on the Saturday afternoon at about three o'clock. According to Charles Hafferty, his mother, his sister, Helen, and her husband, Bill Parker, were already there, and had remained for the rest of the afternoon, until long after the time when Tod Hafferty had met his death.

P.C. Jarrett had informed Inspector Arnold how, later, Marie Hafferty had confirmed this, though he, he had said hastily, intended to double-check with Bill Parker and his wife. Next day, he said. Jarrett went on to relate the rest of what he had learned from Marie

Hafferty; and what Nicky Hafferty had let fly about. Inspector Arnold seemed to agree that Marie Hafferty might prove to be a useful informant, and was worth cultivating.

Jarrett had thought it unnecessary to mention her sexy flirtatiousness; nor did he dwell too much on what Fay Kelly had told him subsequently about her meeting with Nicky Hafferty in Asshe Woods, simply that she had confirmed that they both had an alibi for the relative time that afternoon, was all Jarrett said. He omitted her description of what had occurred between them. He got a good-humoured grunt from the other end of the phone with his account of Alf and Mrs. Layton's alibi.

'So what it adds up to,' Inspector Arnold had said, 'is that Charles Hafferty and his wife appear to be in the clear; so do Alf Layton and his missus — may be something in her having been another of the old boy's little bits of stuff. The Parkers seem okay, too; and Mrs. Hafferty herself — but you're going to check on them personally, the Parkers tomorrow, and the widow soon as you get the doc's okay. Young Nicky Hafferty and Fay Kelly are also accounted for — unless one's covering-up for the other — and there's also Mrs. Kelly to be sorted out, when she's okay to talk. So keep on at it tomorrow, and don't forget that any of those alibis you've got so far aren't all that water-tight. Keep your eyes skinned and ears flapping for anything which may point back at any one of those who seem in the clear. Understand?'

P.C. Jarrett had said he understood, and then Inspector Arnold had suddenly said: 'Did the girl know about her mother carrying on with Hafferty?'

'I don't know,' Jarrett said.

'If she did, she'd hardly be likely to agree to marry the son,' the other had said slowly. 'Even if she's fond of the chap. Of course, we don't know if she is.'

He had paused as if waiting for some comment from Jarrett, but none had come. P.C. Jarrett could only groan inwardly, but he could think of nothing to say. The other went on: 'If she had just turned him down, he might have been in the mood to do something violent. She could have turned him down for financial reasons, of course,' he went on. 'In which case his resentment against his father might have mounted — it may be the old boy was keeping him short of the ready. I think I'd better have a talk with him in the morning. And with the girl too.'

Frank Jarrett had goaned to himself some more. But there was nothing he could do about it. Whatever Inspector Arnold wanted to find out about Fay Kelly and Nicky Hafferty, he would find out all right, and there was damn-all he could do about it.

The other had contributed no further news about how the investigation was going from his end, and had hung up. Jarrett had been left with his ruminations, which were partly concerned with his meeting with the girl on her way to the Parkers' house. Once again he had kept any reference to her out of the case, and he wondered gloomily if he would be forced to add her to the picture after all — after he had found the object of her call on the Parkers. If, he reflected, scowling to himself, they told him.

Shortly afterwards, when his thoughts were switched back to his meeting with Fay Kelly, Oxley had come in, and the two of them had discussed Tod Hafferty's murder and Major Kelly's suicide over supper of bacon-and-eggs. All the time Frank Jarrett had felt a sick sensation at the pit of his stomach every time the name of Fay Kelly came up, and his ears echoed with her account of what had happened between her and Nicky Hafferty in Asshe Woods.

He hadn't felt a very keen appetite for supper, and he had soon taken a cup of coffee into the office and set about writing his reports.

The clock below the mirror said ten minutes past five. It would be two hours yet before pale daylight crept over the windows. He felt the tense, nervous energy of the night-shift worker. His mind went back to his army service; night-patrols, the new meaning time had when everyone else around you was sleeping. He had learned during those two years that food is a good substitute for sleep.

Weariness brings nausea, but if you force yourself to eat, even when the food threatens to choke you, a new kind of strength returns, a mechanical energy which can last for hour after hour.

He had intended to mooch about in his dressing-gown, turning over in his mind all the facts, all the aspects which would point step by step along the road which he foresaw the investigation would take. But now he felt too restless to think things out; he wanted action, he wanted to be moving around. Out there, in the fading darkness lay, he felt, the solution of the enigma. Not here, a chaos of thoughts buzzing around inside his skull.

When he had finished the tea he went quietly back upstairs. He eased open the wardrobe-door so that it wouldn't squeak, and found a pair of trousers and a sports-jacket. He pulled on a sweater. He finished dressing and went downstairs again. Taking an overcoat from the hall he put the catch up on the front door.

It occurred to him that he might take Hero along for company; but then the prospect of having to trudge his way through the grey-lit lanes and along the dull roads depressed him. Better take his bike after all.

As he rode out of the village, he felt that what he was doing had no sense, but a compulsion was driving him as helplessly as a man carried out to sea by a fierce tide. Perhaps this was what detective-work really was, he thought. Perhaps it wasn't meant to run to the routine-pattern he had so far known as a village-cop.

In the dark before the dawn the locale he passed through was shadowy and vague; an orchard that lay alongside the road had the look of a battalion of soldiers lined up, still and waiting.

Jarrett rode on, trying to convince himself that he had some vague idea of taking a look at the chalk-pit again, as if he might find some fresh inspiration there.

It was only as he passed Professor Kane's bungalow and knew that he was approaching Roselands that he could feel his heart racing, and he knew that his entire actions since he had got out of bed had been prompted by a love-sick longing to be as near Fay Kelly as he could. He cursed himself bitterly, as he slowed his bicycle at the sight of the house ahead in the pearly greyness that was beginning to lift the curtain of night at the horizon's edge.

And then he stopped, dismounted and stood waiting in the twin burrowing lights of the car coming his way. Screwing up his eyes against the glare, he could glimpse the familiar low-slung outline behind the giant headlamps. There was the sound of braking, a smooth change-down, and the Duesenberg drew up. A familiar voice said:

'Are you about to make an early morning arrest, P.C. Jarrett?'

'Hello, Dr. Morelle,' the other said, moving out of the headlights' glare and drawing close to the gaunt-faced figure in the driving-seat, whose eyes glinted up at him from under the shadow of his hat-brim. Almost at once he found himself pouring out his account of what had transpired since he had last seen Dr. Morelle.

It was when he mentioned his encounter with the girl that Dr. Morelle interrupted him, with a sudden biting edge to his tone.

'She said she was going to see the Parkers?' he said.

Jarrett nodded, and watched the eyes under the hat-brim narrow in the flare from his cigarette-lighter, as he lit a Le Sphinx.

'The little fool,' he said softly. 'The little fool; I warned her not to try any more tricks like that.'

'What d'you mean, Dr. Morelle?'

'I think you'd better come with me,' was the reply.

Dr. Morelle drove on to Professor Kane's bungalow, Jarrett chasing after him. He left his bicycle, locked and secure, at the back of The Nest, and hurried back to the waiting Duesenberg.

Dr. Morelle said nothing as Jarrett got into the car beside him and he drove off, heading for the road to Richborough's ruined harbour.

Dr. Morelle drove fast along the deserted roads, and P.C. Jarrett sensed the urgency in the way he handled the speeding car. He guessed that they were going to find the girl. He opened his mouth to ask why Dr. Morelle was so certain she would be at the derelict hut on the saltings and not at her home at Eastmarsh, when with that uncanny anticipation which took the policeman's breath away, his unspoken question was answered.

'She was unhappy at home,' Dr. Morelle said. 'There was no love for her there; that is her tragedy. She chose the loneliness of the other place, about which she could weave her own dreams of happiness and security.'

P.C. Jarrett muttered a reply, though he found it confusing to keep up with Dr. Morelle's frightening ability to read his thoughts, even as they were taking shape in his mind.

Now they were racing along the road to Richborough, the wind whipping in from the Goodwins, the pink dawn spreading upwards from beyond the crumbling old castle, more and more swiftly shifting the clouds of night from the sky. Now the

Duesenberg was purring throatily past Bloody Point and the sandhills, and the saltings ran out to the sea, stained with the glistening pale blood reflection of the new morning.

Jarrett's questioning gaze shifted from the figure crouched at the wheel and caught the rusted, towering derricks, tall skeletons straddling the silt; the rotting jetties; the endless miles of straggling, rusted wire. His eyes took in the long, low buildings, forlorn and empty-looking; the troop-barges floundering in the sea of sand and mud, the steel ruins of the forgotten ferry.

The Duesenberg came to a stop. Dr. Morelle got out of the car and strode off swiftly, like some great marsh-bird himself against the backdrop of sea and saltings. It was all P.C. Jarrett could do to keep up with him without actually breaking into a trot. The sense of urgency in that tall, sombre figure reached the policeman like an engulfing wave.

Jarrett followed Dr. Morelle along the sandy path, which widened out into stubble and pebbles. Ahead lay a low, dilapidated hut, for which Dr. Morelle seemed to be making. A bird shot up suddenly, wheeling into the air, crying raucously. Jarrett gave a start, and then followed Dr. Morelle through the doorway of the hut, where the door flapped on one hinge. In the dim light which seeped in from the broken window, P.C. Jarrett made out the jumble of blankets in the shadowy corner.

Dr. Morelle was halfway across the hut, and then he stopped with a jerk. A second's pause and he went forward again more slowly.

Jarrett ran to catch up with him, then he, too, was pulled up with an exclamation.

'The fool,' Dr. Morelle grated between his teeth, as he knelt down beside the figure sprawled there on the overcoat, underneath her strewn glossy film-fan magazines. One had fallen from her limp hand, and Jarrett saw the lurid cover, which featured some scantily clothed sex-symbol, captioned sensationally: Hollywood's Latest Glamour Doll.

Frank Jarrett's gaze swivelled to the figure crumpled up horribly at his feet.

'Her head bashed in,' he breathed: 'Just like Tod Hafferty.'

19

Shortly after he had got to London late that Sunday afternoon, Dr. Morelle had spent the rest of the time in a large office-building in Wardour Street, quiet and somnolent in contrast to its week-day bustle and feverish activity. Even Wardour Street itself was deserted, empty of traffic and pedestrians, and the usual rumble from Oxford Street was muted to a murmur.

It was Inspector Hood, with whom Dr. Morelle had quickly got in touch at his home in Streatham, who had laid it all on. Dr. Morelle had also spoken to the Assistant Commissioner at Scotland Yard, who was down in Surrey for the weekend. The result of it all was that Dr. Morelle had spent the following several hours, watching film after film, or sections of films, in the tiny little projection-theatre, with its comfortable seats and sound-proof walls, of a certain film-company.

There had been further hours spent in one of the film-company's offices, with more discussions with the experts, including those concerned with tape-recording. At last, in the cigarette-smoke haze beneath the strip-lighting that enveloped Dr. Morelle and the fast-talking, precisely thinking shirt-sleeved experts the work was finalized, and he got up from the coffee-cup and cigarette-stub littered desk, went out into the invigoratingly chill early morning that was still dark, with only a hint of the dawn in the air, got behind the wheel of his Duesenberg and headed in a south-east direction.

He had driven fast through the darkness that turned greyer with every mile, anticipating grabbing a few brief hours of sleep at Professor Kane's bungalow, before he could put into operation the plan which had been the object of his night's intense activity.

But, instead there had been that figure with the bicycle in the glare of his headlamps, just as he had reached the end of his journey, with the prospects of that snatched sleep uppermost in his thoughts; and now here he was with P.C. Jarrett beside him, in the derelict hut on the wild saltings that had once been Richborough's old harbour.

Outside a sea-bird cried harshly, as Dr. Morelle knelt by the figure of the girl. P.C. Jarrett stood there swaying slightly, sick to the stomach at the sight. Dr. Morelle stood up slowly.

'Nothing that can be done this side of the grave,' he said.

Jarrett managed to choke back the nausea that rose in his throat, enough to mutter: 'Looks as if she must have died instantly.'

The dark narrowed gaze turned on him probingly. 'And from that what would you deduce?'

Dr. Morelle's voice was rasped with an edge to it that told of his weariness, and his deep horror at what had happened. Almost as if, Jarrett thought, that he held himself to blame, that he ought to have made certain the girl was shielded from the fate she had suffered.

'I — er — I don't understand,' he said.

'You perceive no significance in what

you have noted, that she died swiftly?'

Jarrett shook his head.

'No,' he muttered.

'It indicates,' Dr. Morelle said, 'that either she was taken by surprise,' he glanced towards the door, 'which since that is the only entrance, seems unlikely; or that whoever killed her was no stranger to her, and their visit was not unexpected.'

'Of course,' Jarrett said. 'I can see that, now.' It flashed through his mind that Tod Hafferty had been struck down from behind, which was indicative that his murderer had taken him unawares. 'How long do you think she's been dead?'

'A matter of three or four hours, I would estimate.'

Dr. Morelle decided that the next step was for P.C. Jarrett to remain by the hut, until Sandwich C.I.D. arrived; Dr. Morelle would get on to the telephone to Inspector Arnold from the first call-box he passed on the way back in the Duesenberg to Asshe. After that there was nothing else that he could do, except catch that sleep he had been anticipating, and then prepare his plan for that day, at midday. Jarrett would take his orders as usual from Inspector Arnold.

Dr. Morelle went swiftly off, and within a few moments was driving back the way he had come, without a backward glance at Jarrett's lonely figure silhouetted against the spreading lightness of the sky, where it joined the dark sea.

Dr. Morelle found a call-box halfway to Eastmarsh, and left it to Sandwich police-station to take over; he gave them all the information about what they would find at the hut and then headed the Duesenberg in the direction of Asshe and The Nest. He was about a quarter-of-a-mile from his destination, when he overtook a small car. As he passed it, the driver shouted something and hooted as if signalling him to stop.

Dr. Morelle had caught a glimpse of the figure at the wheel, and recognized him as the local doctor. He slowed down and pulled up as the other came alongside.

A head popped out of the side-window.

'They sent for you, too?' the doctor, a little, rather seedy-looking individual called out.

'What's the trouble?' Dr. Morelle said.

'Bill Parker's wife. He's just phoned me that she's out for the count, with an empty bottle of sleeping-pills by her bed.'

Dr. Morelle followed the other's car, and a few moments later Bill Parker was opening the front-door in answer to the bell. He was wearing a dressing-gown and slippers and his pyjama trousers showed beneath. His face was pasty, eyes staring with shock.

'Thank God you're here,' he gabbled at the little doctor. 'I don't like the look of her at all. Her breathing sounds terrible.'

Abruptly he stopped, staring at Dr. Morelle. In the light from the hall-lamp his face seemed to lose what little colour it had. Then he whirled round on the other. 'If you brought the police in,' he said, 'I consider you've damn well overstepped yourself.'

'He's not the police; this is Dr. Morelle. He just happened to be passing.'

'Oh, I see.' Parker forced a washy smile.

'I'm a bit upset, you understand. No offence meant.'

He led the way up the stairs, the little doctor at his heels. Dr. Morelle waited in the hall while they went up to the bedroom. The door clicked behind them and their voices receded. Dr. Morelle was left with the tick of an ugly grandfather clock to keep him company.

The house showed the average taste of any middle-class, comfortably-off business-man. A small fancy table for the telephone, heavy velvet curtains over the alcove leading through into the sitting-room, a tall standard lamp, wrought-iron base, and contemporary shade modern wallpaper and expensive wall-bracket lights.

A few minutes later, Parker was coming down the stairs, a false, amiable smile on his face. 'I could do with a drink, will you join me?'

Dr. Morelle declined a drink as he followed him into the sitting-room. There was a big, glossy cocktail cabinet in one corner, all glass and highly polished wood. Parker opened it with shaking fingers. The hand that held the glass of whisky he poured himself was shaking. Parker gulped his drink and immediately poured himself another.

Watching him, Dr. Morelle was convinced he was afraid. But afraid of what? His mind went back to the scene in the hut, the sprawled shape lying there in the grey light. 'It's terrible,' Parker was saying wretchedly, 'sitting here wondering how she is.'

'What happened?'

The other shot him a quick look. Then he said: 'My wife said she had a headache and went to bed early. I suggested she might like to sleep in the spare room, then I shouldn't wake her when I got up in the morning. She said it was a good idea.'

This was a pack of lies, Dr. Morelle thought. Whatever reason had decided Parker's wife to sleep in the spare bedroom, it wasn't so that he shouldn't disturb her in the morning. The man's eyes were downcast, he was fiddling with his glass. 'Did she say she was going to take any sleeping-tablets?' he asked.

Parker shook his head. 'She didn't

mention it, but she often suffered from insomnia and she had a bottle of pills the doctor prescribed. I came to bed latish and I lay awake for some time. Even when I got to sleep I slept badly and I woke suddenly, thinking I heard a noise.'

'Was it your wife you'd heard?'

Parker nodded. His face was ghastly pale. 'It was a sort of groan,' he said. 'I got out of bed and rushed into the other room. It was daylight. When I switched the light on I saw at once she was ill. She was a sort of grey colour and her breathing was just awful gasps. I phoned the doctor at once.' Suddenly he put shaking hands up to his face. 'I blame myself,' he said miserably. 'I'll never forgive myself if she dies.'

'You have no reason to blame yourself,' Dr. Morelle said. 'You acted very promptly.'

'You don't understand. When she knew, she just couldn't go on. It's all my fault. It was a complete cave-in.'

Dr. Morelle said nothing; he lit a Le Sphinx and waited quietly while Bill Parker dropped his hands from his face.

'She came to the house. This girl — a local girl. My wife saw her. She told my wife about — about us.'

Dr. Morelle took a drag at his cigarette. He eyed Bill Parker through a cloud of smoke. No need to speak.

'To tell you the truth,' the other was saying, 'I wasn't very happy about it all.' He looked furtively across at Dr. Morelle. 'I'd never been quite sure that I was, well, the only one.'

'You realize what this suggests?'

Parker threw him a nervous glance. He nodded. 'You mean that she might have taken an overdose of sleeping-tablets intentionally?'

They heard footsteps descending, and the doctor appeared at the door. His face told them nothing. 'I'm going to ring for an ambulance,' he said. 'We'd better get her to hospital right away.'

Parker's face was deathly pale. 'Doctor, she won't die, will she?'

'I hope not,' was the reply, and the seedy little man went into the hall and began dialling on the telephone that stood on the ornate little table.

20

The tension in the sitting-room at Asshe House was stretched taut as a violin-string. Bess Pinner bustled in and out, her face pink with excitement, her hands trembling so that the teaspoons rattled in the saucers on the tea-trolley she had brought in, with plates of biscuits.

The clock in the hall struck midday, and Bess clicked her tongue irritably. 'It's six minutes fast,' she said to Miss Frayle, who sat quietly in the corner by the window. 'It always is.'

Miss Frayle smiled at her. Bess bustled out, muttering to herself. A moment later Charles Hafferty came in, followed by Nicky Hafferty, and Miss Frayle found herself comparing the two. They weren't a bit like brothers, she thought. The younger, blond and sulkily good-looking; the elder, slow-moving and stolid.

It was Charles Hafferty who glanced at the tea-trolley, and smiled wryly at Miss

Frayle. 'Bess's way of coping with any crisis,' he said. 'Lashings of tea and biscuits.'

She was about to make some polite reply, when there was a movement at the door and Marie Hafferty stood there. Anger burned across her plump face, and her eyes were narrow with bitterness.

'She's no good to you, Nicky,' she rasped. 'You want to keep away from her.'

Nicky Hafferty had spun round at her.

'What's biting you, this happy morn?' he grinned at her.

'That Kelly bitch is out there,' Marie Hafferty said, 'waiting to throw herself at you. As usual.'

Miss Frayle saw the blond young man's eyebrows shoot up with a faint look of surprise. 'I didn't know you knew so much about my sex-life,' he said genially.

'Sex — that's all you think of,' the woman snarled.

'Who are you to preach?' Nicky sneered.

'I know more than you think I know,' she threw at him.

The other laughed at her. 'And a fat lot

of use it is to you, except fill you with jealousy, jealousy of your own brother-in-law.'

Charles Hafferty said quietly: 'That's enough, Nicky.' He glanced apologetically at Miss Frayle.

'Is that all you can say?' Marie Hafferty turned on her husband 'Can't you even defend me when he says foul things to me?'

He gave her a long slow look, then he deliberately turned his back on her and held out his hands to the fire blazing in the wide fireplace.

Miss Frayle saw Marie Hafferty suddenly go limp, the fire die out of her eyes. She gave a quivering sigh and went and sat down.

Nicky Hafferty growled: 'Where's that damn solicitor?'

As he spoke, Bill Parker came in, eyes heavy from lack of sleep, his chin blue and unshaven. 'Am I late?' he said nervously. 'I came as soon as I could.'

'How is Mrs. Parker getting along?' Miss Frayle asked him.

'Fairly well,' he said. 'But she's very

weak.' He sat down suddenly and his mouth trembled as if he was going to cry.

'You're damned lucky she's alive,' Nicky Hafferty said.

'And that's no thanks to him,' his sister-in-law said.

'Oh, shut up,' he told her. And Miss Frayle caught the look of anguish that flickered across her, betraying her innermost feelings for Nicky Hafferty. Miss Frayle glanced at Marie's husband, but his stolid back was turned to the room as he still bent before the fire. She felt hot with embarrassment for her. How could an adult woman make her feelings appear so obvious, she thought. And especially married as she was to the elder brother. Miss Frayle could not restrain a shudder to herself, and, sickened by that expression on Marie Hafferty's round, pretty face, she turned away to glance out of the window.

She glimpsed P.C. Jarrett's helmet outside the gate, where he was slowly pacing up and down, awaiting, she knew, the arrival of Dr. Morelle, Inspector Arnold, and the Haffertys' family solicitor whom they were bringing over from Sandwich.

Miss Frayle was almost as much in the dark about the reason behind this meeting which had been fixed for midday at Asshe House, as the others who had now all arrived. She had gathered, however, from the few cryptic replies Dr. Morelle had given her that the mystery of Tod Hafferty's murder would be solved that very Monday morning in time to enable Dr. Morelle to drive back to London directly after lunch, to continue his work on the Soho business.

She knew that Dr. Morelle had returned from his London trip in the early hours, to manage with a brief hour's sleep, then Inspector Arnold had arrived at The Nest. Over coffee and toast, plans had been laid. Plans which were linked, it seemed, with the hours Dr. Morelle had spent during the night in Wardour Street; then he and Inspector Arnold had left for Sandwich. All this had transpired while she had been blissfully enjoying breakfast in bed brought her by Professor Kane's house-keeper.

Dr. Morelle, before he had left, had merely advised her that she could be in at the story's climax, if she cared to put in an appearance at Asshe House round about midday.

Miss Frayle's thoughts flickered to P.C. Jarrett and Marie Hafferty's reference to Fay Kelly. She recalled her impression of the girl yesterday, full of apprehension; and there had been that look in the young policeman's face, as if her appearance on the scene was in some way upsetting to him. And it was young Nicky Hafferty's father who had been lying dead in the chalk-pit at that time. Miss Frayle flashed a look at the blond, youthful-looking man. Was there something between him and Fay Kelly? Something to do with his father's murder?

It was fantastic, she thought, the extent of the drama and tragedy which had struck this cut-off rural locality in such a brief space of time. Like one of those sudden and catastrophic whirlwinds which wiped out faraway towns and cities of the East. Tod Hafferty's murder; the suicide of Major Kelly; the murder of the girl in the hut near an old harbour somewhere on the saltings; Mrs. Parker's attempt, unsuccessful as it had turned out, at taking her own life. All this Miss Frayle had gleaned from Dr. Morelle's brief words, plus what Professor Kane had told her. Dr. Morelle had passed on to him news of what had been happening during the past twenty-four hours.

While Miss Frayle's mind grappled with these conjectures, P.C. Frank Jarrett paced up and down outside Asshe House. Only a few minutes before Fay Kelly had stopped the car, which had been her father's, to ask him if Nicky Hafferty had arrived. Jarrett told her that he had, and she had hesitated, and then got out of the car.

'I'll wait for him,' she had said.

'I'm sure he won't be long.'

She had caught his bitter undertone. 'Thank you.' And then, with a quick smile: 'Things aren't really any different than they were a day or two ago, are they? I mean, so far as you're concerned. Whatever had happened, Nicky Hafferty and I would have worked it out together.'

He thought, astonished, here was a girl four or five years younger than he, who was much more mature, readier to accept the reality of life.

'I'm sure he knows nothing about all this dreadful business,' she had said.

But he had not been thinking about that. He was experiencing a lessening of the oppression which had weighed him down. She had been dead right, there was nothing different, so far as he and she were concerned. 'I'm sure it will work out for you,' he said. 'Both of you.'

She had left the car drawn up outside the gates to Asshe House, and gone for a walk. The air was fresh and sunny. She would enjoy the lovely morning, she said. She had certainly got guts, Jarrett had told himself, as he watched her slim figure recede; and then his thoughts had collected round the events of the past few hours.

The discovery of the girl battered to death; the commotion over Mrs. Parker. P.C. Jarrett had been in on the conference between Dr. Morelle and Inspector Arnold, at Eastmarsh police-station, following the

C.I.D.'s arrival at the hut. Jarrett had learned of the dead girl's foolish attempt to blackmail Bill Parker. That was what the light burning late at his office had meant. Jarrett recalled his earlier ideas that Parker was the bottom-pinching type. Well, it had brought his wretched wife to death's door.

As the plan was laid which was to trap Tod Hafferty's and the girl's murderer (it seemed the same person had committed both crimes) Dr. Morelle had been cryptic and, to Jarrett at any rate, bafflingly enigmatic. Dr. Morelle and Inspector Arnold had left Eastmarsh to collect the solicitor at Sandwich, and then the curtain would rise on the last act of the drama.

There was a sudden deep-throated roar, which brought P.C. Jarrett's head up. It was the familiar note of the Duesenberg as it swung into sight and Dr. Morelle changed down. Behind him was Inspector Arnold's police-car, Jarrett moved forward, with a touch at his helmet, his heart starting to race.

21

'These proceedings are unconventional, to say the least,' the solicitor said, over his pince-nez and clearing his throat. 'But, as you may know, he always refused to make an official will, although I urged him to do so. Instead, he put down his last wishes in this form, which, he instructed me, you were all to hear at the earliest possible moment after his death.'

Miss Frayle saw every eye swivel to the tape-recording machine which a plain-clothes man had brought into the room on the heels of Dr. Morelle, Inspector Arnold, and the solicitor, a narrow-faced, sandy-haired man. Charles and Marie Hafferty; Nicky Hafferty and Bill Parker; all of them were on their feet staring at the machine. Miss Frayle caught the expectant look on Inspector Arnold's face. As for Dr. Morelle, his saturnine features were composed almost to the extent of boredom. But that was to be expected of him, Miss Frayle knew. Never a sign from him that he was experiencing the slightest sensation of interest, although this whole business had been his idea. The solicitor had been well briefed on the job he had to do.

'It is unfortunate,' the latter was murmuring, in suitably sympathetic tones, 'that both the widow and Mrs. Parker are unable to be present; but they will, of course, have an opportunity to hear it all at their convenience. In any case those were his instructions and I must follow them. Has anyone else any comments, or may I proceed?'

'Get on with it,' Nicky Hafferty growled. 'We haven't got all day.'

Miss Frayle saw Dr. Morelle's glance rake the blond young man's face. Dr. Morelle's eyes were narrowed, and a tingle of excitement began crawling down Miss Frayle's spine. Nicky Hafferty was trying to look impatient at the whole business. No one else spoke. Marie Hafferty seemed to edge further away from her husband, who stood there, his expression stolid and faintly worried. Bill

Parker was chewing at his thumbnail. Overhead, Miss Frayle caught a sound, no doubt someone moving about in Mrs. Hafferty's bedroom.

'Very well then,' the solicitor was saying, clearing his throat once more. 'I shall now switch on the machine.' His voice was high and precise. 'When you listen to this you will be hearing Tod Hafferty's own voice, speaking his own words.'

There was a click as the plain-clothes detective touched the switch. There followed a hissing noise as the spool of recording-tape started turning, and then a warm, vibrant voice filled the tense, silent room. 'I don't imagine many of you will be sorry, except Helen, my dearly beloved, when I hand in my chips,' Tod Hafferty began. 'None of you have done much for me, so you won't find I've done a lot for you, either.'

There was a rustle of resentment round the room. Or was it dismay, Miss Frayle wondered? The solicitor looked upset; only Marie Hafferty had a slight smile. The others were frowning to themselves.

The solicitor cleared his throat as Tod Hafferty's voice continued. 'I've made a lot of money in my time, and here's what I've done with it. Asshe House is for Helen, with a thousand a year for its upkeep. Charles is okay, with the house I've given him. And that's his lot.' There was a gasp from Marie Hafferty and her husband's features had darkened.

'Now for the money,' the richly-toned voice went on. 'Five thousand pounds is to go to my daughter Olivia, to be put into a private account in her name. Whatever happens, it isn't to go into the joint account she runs with her precious husband.' There was a vicious snarl from Bill Parker. 'Ten thousand pounds to my wife, Helen, which should see she wants for nothing for the rest of her days. As for the rakehell son of mine, Nicky, well, perhaps he'll pull himself together, though I doubt it, but I leave five thousand pounds to him, to give him a chance.'

'Who'd have thought it of the old devil,' Nicky Hafferty muttered. And then: 'Wait till I tell this to Fay.'

The machine went silent and at a signal from the solicitor, the plain-clothes man switched it off. 'There must be something else,' Marie Hafferty said loudly. 'What about me? He must have left something to me.' Her voice had become a half-sob, half-scream. She put her hand to her mouth and Miss Frayle saw her bite hard on the fleshy part of her thumb. Her face was paper white.

Her husband said roughly: 'What the devil's got into you? There's no reason why Tod should have left you a penny. Me, yes, but I'm not surprised. He said a long time ago I'd have to make what I could out of my job.'

Nicky Hafferty laughed out loud. Marie whirled on him, her eyes glittering. 'Shut up, you rat. I suppose you'll go off whoring with Fay Kelly now.'

Charles Hafferty grabbed her arm. 'Don't talk like that, I won't have it.'

'You won't have it.' She jerked her arm free. 'Do you think I care what you'll have and what you won't have?'

He stared stupidly at her. 'What's got into you? Why did you think Tod might leave anything to you?'

'I'll tell you why.' It was Nicky who spoke. Her jeer had infuriated him. 'Because she did what she talks about so prettily. She went whoring with Tod.' He gave a short laugh at the stunned horror on his brother's face. 'Yes, your wife and your own father. Makes you sick, doesn't it? That's why she thought she'd get his money. Because she slept with him for it.'

She slapped Nicky Hafferty's face so hard it was like the crack of a whip. He half fell back, then he made as if to go for her with the light of murder in his eyes. Then his brother pushed him aside and faced his wife.

'I didn't want to do it,' she said. 'Tod was nothing to me, but he found me exciting.'

Shock and horrified embarrassment struggled on her husband's face, as he reeled like an axed tree that requires only a touch from the woodsman to send it crashing down. No one else moved. Miss Frayle's glance sought Dr. Morelle, but he leaned negligently against the corner of the low writing-desk. The next action came from Inspector Arnold, who was suddenly very close to Marie Hafferty, as he said to Charles Hafferty: 'Where was your wife on Saturday afternoon?'

He blinked at the detective. 'Here, of course,' he said. 'Here with me.'

'She came with you?'

'You know that my wife and I were here together.'

'But you came ahead of her,' Inspector Arnold said quietly. 'Now you come to think of it, isn't that the case? Mrs. Hafferty was delayed, she didn't arrive here until about forty minutes after you — '

'What are you driving at — ?' But his whole face seemed to have sagged, as the other's words struck home.

As Miss Frayle could feel her heart racing in her throat, Inspector Arnold turned and nodded to the plain-clothes detective. There was a click and the hiss of the tape in the recording-machine sounded one more. Then Tod Hafferty's vibrant tones filled the room.

'That's why you murdered me, my girl . . . To get my money . . . And all the time it wasn't there . . . You, who were only one of dozens, why should I leave you a penny?'

With a dreadful cry, Marie Hafferty hurled herself at the machine and sent it crashing from the table on which it had been placed. She spun round like a wild-cat and went through the room, leaving Inspector Arnold and the plain-clothes detective racing after her. They hit Bess Pinner head on. She looked flustered, caught out eavesdropping. Inspector Arnold cursed and thrust her out of the way. There came the roar of a car-engine starting up outside.

Dr. Morelle moved after them as they ran down the path to the front gate. The car Fay Kelly had left there, while she had gone for a walk, was streaking down the road, crashing through the gears.

Inspector Arnold was calm, business-like. 'Get on the phone,' he told P.C. Jarrett, who was still trying to grasp what had happened. 'General alert. Small, black car. Know the number?'

Jarrett nodded, and thrust his way through those hurrying out of the house.

Inspector Arnold said to the plain-clothes man: 'She won't get far.' The two men bustled into the police-car with the uniformed driver at the wheel. Inspector Arnold called out to Nicky Hafferty, his blond hair tousled with excitement: 'What sort of a driver is she?'

'Rotten. She hasn't got her licence. Too damned reckless.'

As the police-car shot forward, Inspector Arnold grunted to the driver: 'If Jarrett's got through on the blower, her little joyride will soon be over. Step on it, I'd like to be in at the kill.'

A few minutes later he said softly: 'There she is.' The black car was crawling, it seemed, along the ribbon-like road a mile ahead. Inspector Arnold showed some excitement. 'Come on,' he growled to the uniformed figure at the wheel. 'Can't you get any more out of this old heap?'

The police-car was too far behind, but close enough for Inspector Arnold and the two others to see it happen. Marie Hafferty must have seen the other police-car, one that had been alerted from

Sandwich, appear out of a turning ahead and turn to bear down on her. There was no chance for her to turn off. Whether it was panic or bravado they never knew. She slewed the wheel over and screamed across the road into a brick wall. The car disintegrated.

Inspector Arnold stumbled out of the police-car and went at a run to the tangled mess by the side of the road. He saw Marie Hafferty at once and turned away, sickened. As the policemen from the other car came rushing up, he waved a hand. 'You don't have to hurry,' he shouted. 'It's all over.'

Back at Asshe House, Miss Frayle had left Charles Hafferty in the sitting-room, talking in a stunned manner to Dr. Morelle. She found her way to the Duesenberg, where she sat, waiting for Dr. Morelle to drive back to Professor Kane's, before returning to London. She had seen Nicky Hafferty and Fay Kelly wander off through the garden at the side of the house, while Bill Parker was on the telephone inquiring at the local hospital about his wife.

P.C. Jarrett, having alerted Sandwich, was pacing up and down outside the house. Miss Frayle saw him touch his helmet to Dr. Morelle, as he came out of the gate. She heard Dr. Morelle say: 'I am returning to Professor Kane's bungalow, where Inspector Arnold can find me for the next hour.'

'Yes, Dr. Morelle.'

'Then I shall be leaving for London. Mr. Charles Hafferty will await Inspector Arnold's return.' And Dr. Morelle was moving swiftly to the Duesenberg. As he got into the driving-seat, Miss Frayle said:

'I don't understand; I mean, she'd murdered Tod Hafferty, because he'd promised to leave her some money, or she thought he had, but, why did she murder that girl as well?'

'The fool was trying to blackmail her; she knew about Marie Hafferty's illicit relationship with her father-in-law. She told me that herself, and I warned her, but she wouldn't listen. She tried to blackmail Bill Parker's wife, who attempted to commit suicide. Marie Hafferty reacted somewhat differently. She found her at the hut, and silenced her.'

'The one I'm sorry for is that poor husband of hers,' Miss Frayle said, stifling a shudder.

Dr. Morelle lit a Le Sphinx. 'He has just admitted to me what I had suspected all along. He saw the body in the chalk-pit the first time he went out to search with the policeman, Jarrett, and felt convinced then that his wife had killed him. He slipped back afterwards,' Dr. Morelle said, 'and confirmed that he was dead.' Dr. Morelle was reversing the Duesenberg in order to return to The Nest.

'Did he know she had also murdered the girl?' Miss Frayle asked.

Dr. Morelle replied that Charles Hafferty, experiencing an inexplicable anxiety concerning his wife, had come over from Asshe House, in time to see her riding off on a bicycle. He had waited for her to come back, which she did over an hour later. Unknown to her, he had heard her in the bathroom. He had waited until she had gone to bed, and had found the coat she had been wearing stained with blood, which she had not entirely washed off.

Miss Frayle sighed deeply.

As Dr. Morelle stopped the car outside Professor Kane's bungalow, she heard herself blurting out the strange coincidence of the dream, or nightmare, in the dentist's chair. When she asked him to explain how it was that Tod Hafferty's name had arisen, Dr. Morelle turned his glance on her, darkly sardonic. Then he handed her something from under the dash. It was a crumpled piece torn from a magazine. It was a photograph of Tod Hafferty.

As she stared at it she heard him saying: 'You dropped it during our drive down from London on Saturday night.'

She started to ask him how she could possibly have come by it, when recollection swept her back to the dentist's waiting room; as clearly as if she was there again she recalled opening a glossy film-magazine and finding to her surprise, one page half-torn out as if by a child. Only a photograph of Tod Hafferty, as he had appeared in some romantic role when in his prime, remained. It was a handsome profile, and it had reminded her of Dr. Morelle. She could feel herself blushing, as the memory came back to her: how on a sudden impulse she had carefully removed it and pushed it into her handbag.

'At least it served some purpose,' Dr. Morelle was murmuring, as he opened the car-door to get out. 'It suggested to me the idea by which Marie Hafferty confessed her guilt.'

She looked from the photo fragment in her hand to him, her eyes behind her horn-rims questioning.

'The police learned from the solicitor, during the course of their inquiries,' Dr. Morelle said, 'of Tod Hafferty's tape-recorded substitute for a will. The last part, in which he denounced Marie Hafferty, was added to it.'

'How?'

'Made up from parts of dialogue from various films in which he had appeared,' Dr. Morelle said. 'Grafted, so to speak, on the end of the tape. Something of a technical achievement, don't you agree?'

But Miss Frayle, even as she began to grasp what he was saying, found her thoughts suddenly switched to the image of that desperate woman, screaming her head off, as she raced out of the room, and she felt a sudden intuition that Marie Hafferty would never live to be tried for her two dreadful crimes.

She started to say something to that effect, then she caught that glance turned to her, impatiently awaiting her fulsome praise for his brilliant idea.

Miss Frayle changed her mind and began telling Dr. Morelle how marvellously clever he was.

We do hope that you have enjoyed reading this large print book.

Did you know that all of our titles are available for purchase?

We publish a wide range of high quality large print books including:
Romances, Mysteries, Classics
General Fiction
Non Fiction and Westerns

Special interest titles available in large print are:
The Little Oxford Dictionary
Music Book, Song Book
Hymn Book, Service Book

Also available from us courtesy of Oxford University Press:
Young Readers' Dictionary
(large print edition)
Young Readers' Thesaurus
(large print edition)

For further information or a free brochure, please contact us at:
Ulverscroft Large Print Books Ltd.,
The Green, Bradgate Road, Anstey,
Leicester, LE7 7FU, England.
Tel: (00 44) **0116 236 4325**
Fax: (00 44) **0116 234 0205**